Nasty
DICK

DEX

Nasty D!ck

Published by:
Just Dex Publishing
18530 Mack Ave. Suite, 178
Grosse Pointe, Mich 48236
MySpace.com/JustDexPublishing
E-Mail: Dex33@Comcast.net

ISBN-10: 0-97782022X

Nasty D!ck
Revised by DEX
Edited by Mike Lee and DEX
Text formation by DEX
Cover concept by: Midknight Graphx

Kitty Kat

C'mon Dex. Wheelie the whole block," said Binky.

"Yeah, Dex! Do it, man," encouraged a slew of other neighborhood kids. Sitting in the middle of the street on his bike, Dex felt the energy of the cheering crowd.

"I ain't wheelie this bike in about five or six years, but I still got it, never lost it. I can do this!" he voiced aloud, even though he'd never before attempted such a distance. Dex then laid eyes on Flower, who'd just turned fifteen and was shaping up very well. She gave him a smile and blew a kiss. He did the same in return, but those wind kisses were getting old. Dex was sixteen; hot and horny in the ass. This virgin was tired of jacking off and flipping through magazines. He wanted sex; whether it was oral, anal or missionary, he was willing to accept it from whatever woman that was willing to give it.

Dex's other neighborhood partners, Derrick, Leroy, and Freddy were there cheering him on, too.

Damn, everybody's watching, somewhat feeling the pressure.

Dex was about to ride to his starting point when a hand clutched his shoulder. He turned to look. It was his right-hand man, Coco-Mo. "Oh, what's up, Coco-Mo?" he greeted.

Coco-Mo frowned. "Dex, what I tell you 'bout that Coco-Mo shit? The name is *Coke,* man, just Coke. Coco-Mo sounds like some type of damn weed plant."

Dex shrugged his shoulders.

Coke was a seventeen year old kid who never smiled. He wasn't the type to start some shit, but was skilled at bringing shit to an abrupt end. He did more listening than he did talking. Coke was a person who watched and studied the moves and the mistakes of the older male figures in his family. Often when adults encountered the company of Coke, they called him an old soul who's been here before.

Coke continued, "So you're about'a show your ass, huh? You gon' let these youngsters geek you up to wheelie a whole block, right?"

"Yup," responded Dex, riding around Coke in circles.

"Okay bad ass, go ahead then, but when you get your ass laid out in that street like a rug, don't look for me to help you off the ground."

Dex continued prancing as if he had no worries. At the same time he had again locked eyes with Flower. She and Dex had been friends every since they could remember, but the two were now starting to take interest in one another. Coke peeped it.

"Oh... you're showin' out for that broad over there again, huh? I told you before Dex, she's nothing but a tramp; she's not the one for you. That girl there is gon' be your downfall."

Dex laughed. "Don't be jealous Coke, man. Just get a life. See you in a minute," he said, riding off to his starting point.

Dex reached the corner, planting his foot on the pavement. Strangely, his shoe began sliding sideways. He looked down and noticed an oil slick in the street. "Dang!" He dragged the soles of his shoes back and forth along the grass.

It was now time to ride. The midnight blue and gray Schwinn Stingray stood ready as if it was a stunt cycle. Accessorized with chrome mirrors, horns, colored straps, and crash pads, it was a sight to see. *Bike seven years old and still looks damn good.*

Dex

Finally, Dex took off. He gathered some speed and pulled back on the handlebars. He was now up and riding on the back wheel, simultaneously braking and peddling to maintain his speed.

Within fifteen seconds, he'd broken his old record by completing half a block. The roaring crowd could be heard just up ahead. Suddenly, Dex felt his shoe slipping from the pedal. *Uh oh...*, knowing he didn't get all the oil off his shoes. To regain his footing, he had to pedal faster, but the faster he pedaled, the less he was in control.

A concerned Flower pointed. "Dex is going too fast," as she observed his approach. Coke agreed.

"Naw, he planned it this way," assured Freddy. Everyone else wasn't so sure.

Just then, Dex flew by them all. A wind tunnel followed. The sight of his front wheel twisting from left to right, along with his huffing jaws told the real story.

Dex was barely in control, but determined, nonetheless, to finish what he started. With only three house lengths from his goal, a smirk appeared across his face. *I'm the sweetest ever.*

Suddenly, a green sedan wildly bent the corner. In a panic, Dex hit the brakes, as did the charging vehicle, but it was too late. The bike's front tire collided with the car's front bumper. The force launched Dex into the air like a scud missile. Within seconds, he crashed back down onto the car's windshield. *Bbooosssshhh!* The driver came to a screeching halt, throwing Dex across the hood and into the street.

In shock, Flower covered her mouth with her hands, screaming. "Oh Lord! Oh Lord!"

Freddy was walking in circles holding his face. *He's dead. Dex's dead. He killed him.* Derrick, Leroy, Binky, and the others ran towards the scene.

Nasty D!ck

"Oh shit!" exclaimed the driver standing behind the driver's door, thinking he had killed the youngster, but to his relief, the young man was moving.

At that point, Dex turned over and made eye contact with the man who hit him. Coke took a long, hard look, as well. The man looked to be twenty-one or twenty-two years old. He had sandy brown hair, a thin mustache, and a high yellow, pinkish complexion, appearing to be Albino. He was approaching Dex, when he saw and heard the angry mob of teens running toward him, screaming.

"You killed him! He's Dead! You killed Dex!"

Fearing his own safety, the man jumped back into his car, and slammed it in reverse, dragging the mangled bike wedged underneath with it. The large sedan then bent the corner and sped away, leaving remains of the bike behind. Derrick, Leroy, Binky, and the rest approached Dex.

"Damn, Dex, are you okay? Are you alright? Are you bleeding?" were the most frequently asked questions.

Dex said nothing. He just lay with his mouth open, rocking back and forth, holding his nuts, trying to regain some feeling. When he landed on the windshield, it was ass first, scissoring his balls between his thighs. The pain was excruciating.

Realizing there wasn't a serious injury, four-foot tall Binky found humor in Dex's mishap. He then exchanged glances with Leroy and Derrick. The two looked away, grinning. The others began to chuckle themselves, but not Freddy. He knew better. He knew a side of Dex that none of the others could even begin to imagine. Coke took a head count of those who were laughing. Right then, Flower stepped in.

Dex

"What y'all laughing at? This shit ain't funny! That's my man lying there! Dex supposed to be y'all friend. Don't just stand there, help him home!" she shouted.

Even though Freddy was the first to assist, he despised Flower's claims of being Dex's woman. Derrick, Leroy and Binky also helped grabbing each one of Dex's legs and arms, assisting Freddy to carry him home.

Arriving at the housing complex, Flower rang the doorbell. When the door opened, all eyes and mouths popped wide open. It was as if a sculptor had chiseled the perfect masterpiece and breath life into it and set it free.

There stood Catwalk, twenty-seven years old. She was five-foot-six, full-breasted, slim in the waist, and pretty in the face; a true goddess with full lips and stallion hips. Her ass was so big it could be seen from the front. Freddy and the rest of the boys grew erect. Flower placed her hands on her hips.

"Who are you? And where's Miss Chandler?" she asked, with attitude.

Catwalk replied, defensively. "What, lil girl? Who you think you talkin'…!"

Catwalk cut her statement short when she caught a glimpse of an injured Dex, grunting in pain. She sprinted off the two-step porch in her stilettos. She knelt down and checked him for injuries.

"Are you okay? Where are you hurt baby?" she asked, while caressing his face. "What happened?" she looked to Freddy and the other boys.

They were all too stunned to answer. Their eyes were glued on the deep, bulging cut that separated her breasts.

Man... she's pretty. I wish she was my momma, thought Binky.

7

Nasty D!ck

Flower intervened. "What do you think happened, lady? Just look at his bike," pointing to the mangled wreck being dragged up the walkway.

Like a dumb blonde, Catwalk was still puzzled. Flower saw that she had to spell it out.

"Duh...! Dex got hit by a car," thinking, *Stupid bitch!* Catwalk's eyes widened. "Hit by a car! Oh my God! Bring him in the house," she ordered.

Inside the house, the boys flopped Dex on the couch like a rag doll. "Ooofff!" he groaned, but there was no sympathy coming from the four man juvenile crew. Their hormones were raging, as they all watched in lust as Catwalk scurried back and forth across the hardwood floor. Her ass, breasts, and hips were a feast for their eyes.

In a frenzy, she grabbed an ice pack, bandages, cotton gauze, tape, scissors, tweezers, anti-bacterial cream, burn cream, aspirin, and some butterfly stitches. She was now ready for surgery. It clearly was an overreaction. The boys found it to be hilarious.

Flower just shook her head, thinking, *This woman ain't got no good sense.*

Finally, Dex gathered the breath to explain his injury to Catwalk. She smirked. "Oh...why didn't you say so before Dex?" She went into the kitchen and returned with a plastic baggie of ice. "Now, show me where you're hurt."

Dex pointed through his pants to his testicles. "Right here," while gritting his teeth.

"No, show me," she insisted.

Dex's eyebrows lifted. *Show you? Okay...*
Thinking nothing of it, Dex unzipped his pants, exposing his underwear. "Right here," he again pointed. "This is where it hurts."

Dex

But Catwalk gave him a look that again spoke, *Show me.*

Dex was floored. He was a private guy. The only other woman to ever see him naked was his mother, and that was years ago. The decision was puzzling, a difficult one to make, so he looked to his partners for some advice. Coke gave his consent with a thumbs up. Freddy, Leroy, Binky and Derrick gave no objections, either. The smiles on their faces were their approvals, but Flower's tight lips and squinting eyes said something altogether different, almost to say: *Show that woman your dick, and I'll cut it off.* That evil eye helped Dex make up his mind.

"Catwalk," he called out in pain. "I'm hurtin' real bad, but I can't show you my privates. At least not in front of them," he grunted, pointing to everyone else in the room.

Catwalk stood from the couch. "Okay y'all, it's time to roll."

Flower's face bent up. "Time to roll! I ain't goin' nowhere! That's my man, and this ain't yo' house! Dex, she just wanna see yo' di..," but before Flower could finish, Freddy muzzled her mouth.

Now on a rampage, Flower had to be physically restrained. The boys had no idea she was so strong. After about two minutes of struggling and repeated warnings to Dex not to trust Catwalk, she was rushed out of the house like a violent protestor.

Catwalk slammed the front door and returned to the couch. "Damn! I'm glad I'm not a man, so I don't have to deal with bitches like that, shit! You need to leave that girl alone, Dex. She ain't gon' do nothin' but give you hell."

"Yeah, I know, and I'm sorry for Flower's outbursts. She has a slight temper problem, but she's really a sweet girl," commented Dex.

9

Nasty D!ck

"Sweet? Maybe when she's asleep, but you are right, she's very much so a girl, and that's all she is. She doesn't have a clue for what it takes to fix up an injured groin. Shoot, I got ten years experience as a Nurse's Aid, don't play with me. I done seen stab wound, people shot and dead bodies. And the nerve of her telling you not to trust me, I'm practically family. Me and your uncle Goose have been dating for three weeks already. We talkin' 'bout getting married. I love him so… much. But anyway Dex, with your cute self, show me again where you're hurting."

Dex thought she would never ask. The throbbing pain diminished whatever embarrassment he thought he may have felt exposing himself. He then lowered his underwear, pulling himself out. His penis lay on his thigh like a great whale washed ashore.

Catwalk's eyes widened. "Oh my God! I mean, lift your penis," catching herself. "I need to sit this ice pack on your testicles."

Dex did as instructed, lifting himself. The ice gave relief on contact. "Aahhh…" he sighed.

Catwalk was in thought. *Lord, have mercy. This boy got a-dick-on-him, and I thought his uncle had it goin' on. Just look at it; sittin' there all pretty, thick and long with a mushroom head, and it ain't even hard yet. Mmmph! I see why that girl was having a fit. She couldn't handle all that dick no way, but I know somebody who can.*

Katrina Bryant, AKA Catwalk, was a freak. A seductive woman who preyed on the kindness of men to get what she wanted. Most times it was for financial gain, other times it was to satisfy her nympho-like appetite. She and Goose, Dex's uncle, who lived with him and his mother, Barbara Chandler, met a few weeks ago in a beauty supply store. After purchasing some silk scarves to wrap his pump-waves hairdo, Goose noticed Cupid's devil strolling up and down the aisle ways. He then stepped to Catwalk and began a conversation. Goose often used his celebrity status to gain leverage with the ladies. He belonged to a dance group entitled: The Five Horsemen, who lip-synched their performances at hair shows around the country, so he was accustomed to women falling to their knees.

After a few rolls in the hay with Catwalk, The ladies man, Player, and Mack, Goose considered himself to be had met his match. He never before had a woman do the things to him like Catwalk did. She fucked him, sucked him, and licked his balls, ass, ears, fingertips, and toes. He loved when she kissed and licked the crack of his ass, up his back, to his neck and around his throat. The woman was a nasty freak. So nasty, that one night Goose came in her mouth while receiving a head job. Afterwards, the two share the rewards through a kiss.

Catwalk lifted the ice pack, checking the status of Dex's injury. "Looks like the swelling is going down," she stated crossing her legs, easing closer. Then out of nowhere, "Do you like me, Dex? Do you like older women?" she asked.

"Huh? What?" Dex was confused. He didn't understand where Catwalk was coming from. She was supposed to have been his uncle's new girl, but before he could offer her any response, Catwalk dived face first into his lap. Dex stiffened immediately.

Having never felt a warm mouth around his dick, Dex gasped. "W-what you doin'?"

"Shut the fuck up and lay on back," she said, forcefully pinning him to the couch. "I'm 'bout'a make you a man."

Nasty D!ck

Dex wasn't sure if that's what he wanted or not, but the feeling was exhilarating, way better than sneaking his uncle's porno flicks.

Catwalk was sucking fast and hard, knowing she didn't have much time. Goose was on a simple cigarette and Pepsi run to the store.

"That dick gon' bust for me. Kitty Kat gon' make that dick bust!" she seductively spoke, slapping his dick up against her tongue and jaw. She then tried several times to deep throat the teenaged adolescent down to his nuts, but that was proving itself to be a challenge. She gagged and coughed again and again. A vein suddenly appeared in the middle of her forehead. Dex began to feel a little sorry for Catwalk.

"Maybe we ought'a stop," he insisted, ready to pull up his pants. "I mean ..."

Catwalk looked up, giving Dex a cold stare. "Maybe we ought'a stop?" *I just know this young boy don't think he did something, 'cause I choked on his dick a couple of times? He must think I can't handle him. This boy ain't ready for me.*

At that moment, Catwalk peeled off her spandex pants that, so tightly, hugged her shapely figure. She then popped her bra, and pulled up her shirt.

Dex couldn't believe it. *I'm looking at pussy, ass, and titties on a grown woman; first a blowjob, and now this?* It was the moment for so long Dex had been waiting for, but it was too much, too fast for the virgin. He felt this wasn't right. "Catwalk."

"Shhhhh...," expressed Catwalk, placing her finger on Dex's lips. She didn't want to hear any more talking. At this point, it was all about her. She now felt she had to prove herself. With her stilettos still on, she straddled Dex's waist.

Dex

"Oooohhhh... eeewwww... wait a minute, wait a min..." moaned Dex on contact, feeling himself tingle, already feeling like he wanted to cum. He firmly held Catwalk by her waistline, as she long stroked his slick penis. He starred, watching her pink cookie melt down onto his chocolate wafer. The sight was surreal never before witnessed by his lusting eyes, a new chapter to be written in his life story history book.

Catwalk's pussy was already soaking wet. Sucking a dick always made her that way. As she seesaw up and down on Dex's pole, she could feel him throbbing through her wetness. She then curled her lips. "What's the matter, Dex? Why you sounding like that?" as if she didn't know. Next, she leaned in to nibble on his ear, while at the same time, grinding on his dick.

Dex was breathing like he was blowing out candles trying to fight the feeling. The pussy was like nothing he'd ever felt before. He could feel the numbness setting in his hands, now traveling the length of his spine. *What's the matter with me?* confused and a little scared. Suddenly, Dex arched his back, tightly, gripping her hips.

"Uhhh...," he moaned, feeling the shock waves through his body, filling her glass with warm milk. Afterwards, a drizzle of saliva escaped his lips, leaving him in a paralytic state.

Catwalk squint her eyes. *I know my pussy is good. I got his young ass now, but I must admit this boy is filling me up. He's hittin' all my spots. Whew! I done came twice already. This dick is good, but I ain't about'a bow down to it. Get him girl, ride that dick!*

Because he was still rock hard, Catwalk had no idea Dex had just came. He was coming off the natural high,

Nasty D!ck

dizzy feeling a good nut gave off. For him, this was round two.

Dex slid himself downward on the couch, positioning her body over him like he was a chair. He then gripped her ass and began thrusting upwards, pulling her down on every inch of him. He was intrigued by how she moaned every time he pushed deep inside. The seductive sounds and rhythm of the slapping bodies intensified the sex.

Catwalk squeezed her breast. "Uh...! Oh, my God! You're fuckin' me so... good. You young muthafucka! Give that dick-to-me. Fuck me Dex!"

Dex forcefully, obliged.

Just then, the front door opened. Goose walked in smoking a cigarette, closing the door behind him. He pointed to the outside ready to speak on Dex's mangled bike, when the look on Catwalk's face puzzled him.

"Damn, baby, why you looking like that? You got that look on your face like when I be fuckin' you," unable to see Dex who was slumped down on the couch. "You know that look turns me on, makes my dick hard. You sure everything cool?" he asked, walking into the kitchen, still eyeing her from the archway view in the dining room wall.

Catwalk was frozen with fear. She'd lost track of time during her sexual encounter. Having no idea what to do, she nodded, saying, "Everything's fine," shifting her eyes downward to Dex.

Dex had the, *What we gon' do?* look on his face. *Who you asking?* Catwalk's facial expression frowned in response.

By this time, Goose had taken off his shirt and was now pulling off his pants, never taking an eye off Catwalk. Her seductive look had him ready to fuck.

Dex

"Whew, you turn me on. You know I love your sexy ass, right baby?" he stated, while stroking his penis. He began walking towards the couch. "C'mon, baby. Gimme a quickie real fast. Dex is outside and Barbara will be here any..." Goose was stopped in his tracks. Nerve needles pricked his face.

"I'm sorry, Goose baby," said Catwalk, hopping off Dex. "But it ain't what you think."

"Well, what the fuck is it then, bitch! Explain the shit to me!" he yelled, enraged, looking at her and Dex's naked bodies.

Dex stood up, pulling up his pants.

"Uncle Goose, I... uh... she..."

"Uh, uh, Dex, don't even worry 'bout it. This ain't your fault. This bitch knows exactly what she was doing. Don't you bitch!" snatching Catwalk by the back of her hair, throwing her on the couch, pointing his fingers in her face.

"I knew you were a trifling hoe when I first saw you. And to think, I was about'a marry yo' ass. I slipped myself this time. That's alright, though, I got something for trifling hoes!"

Right then, Goose bent Catwalk over the couch. He spit in his hand to wet her pussy and started drilling her, mercilessly. He pulling her hair and slapping her ass as if he was riding a horse, all in front of Dex.

"Yeah, you like that, huh? You like that shit, don't you bitch? Tell me you like it!"

Dex was embarrassed. He covered his face feeling like this was somehow his fault, but when he heard, "Yes, daddy, I like it. Fuck me good. This is yo' pussy," he was floored.

Catwalk was submissive to his uncle's verbal abuse. He also noticed that Goose was turned on by the fact that

Nasty D!ck

Catwalk had sex with someone else. This was strange to Dex, but he would come to understand this behavior in time.

"C'mon, nephew!" called Goose. "Stick yo' dick in her mouth. Let's run a train on this bitch!"

Dex didn't have to be told twice. He kicked off his shoes, and pulled down his pants, but just as he took off his underwear, his mother Barbara walked in from work.

Dex shook his head toward the floor, smiling.

"That was a hellu'va good *and* bad day," he said to Dr. Barton, sitting on the patients couch. "My momma was mad as hell. She put all of our asses out of the house. She called Catwalk a trashy whore with no self-respect, Goose a raggedy ass, broke ass, wanna be Player. And me? She couldn't find any words for me. It was just disappointment written across her face. Shit, Doc, she even threw the couch out and burned it. My momma was pissed," he laughed.

Dr. James Barton was intrigued by all of Dex's sexual tales. Even though he was financially well off from his profession, he didn't have the know-how or charisma to get women to do half of the things he was hearing about. He again found himself in a passionate zone picturing the vivid story.

"Ahem! Ahem!" he sounded, clearing his throat, getting back into his professional mode. "So, Dex, from your early sexual experiences we've covered in our counseling sessions, do you personally feel or believe these issues have had some type of affect on your adult life?"

"Hell yeah!" answered Dex, having no doubt. You already know most of my story, Doc. I'm fucked up and freaked out. I'll suck a fat coochie until it pops. I'll split and lick a clit until it creams with cum, then jump on it and drill that ass, no matter her situation. Like my uncle Goose used to say, 'If you can walk through mud, you can fuck through blood.' You know me, doc. I goes hard on them broads," holding his hand out for a five.

Dr. Barton gave a faint grin, pointing with his pen, as if to say, *You're the man.* "But no, Dex, let me rephrase the question," said the doctor, scribbling on his notepad. "Do you have any regrets today that pertain to your past?"

Dex got up from the chair and took a deep breath. He strolled over to the window, looking out over the Detroit River across to Canada. At times he wished he was a bird and could just fly away from his problems. Discussing his problems with Dr. Barton was therapeutic for him. He got to express his feelings and discuss whatever issues that were on his mind.

Most times, they talked about the absence of his father in his life, but there were other issues, still in the dark. Dex sat back in the chair.

"Yeah doc, I do have one regret from back in the day. I mean, don't get me wrong. I wouldn't change anything about my life, but if I could go back to 1988, I would handle things differently with Flower than I did."

Right then, Dex went in to the story about how hurt Flower was behind the news of he and Catwalk's sexual relations. He explained to Dr. Barton he only told two people about their encounter: Coke and Freddy, his two best friends. Dex said he was sure Coke didn't say anything to Flower because the two didn't associate, so that left only Freddy, who always had a wandering eye for Flower, now that he thought about it.

Freddy repeatedly denied discussing any of the information with Flower that was disclosed to him, but

Nasty D!ck

Flower was more than sure of the story to be true when she spoke of it to Dex.

"We remained a couple for about a year after that. But check this out Doc, two years after our breakup, why did Freddy and Flower secretly marry and have a baby?" eyeing Dr. Barton. "I dated that girl for five years and didn't fuck her one time, let alone have a kid with her. That's what I regret, ol' stankin' bitch! She always talkin' 'bout, 'My body is my sacred temple, Dex. Respect my wishes and don't violate my innocence.' Her innocence! Bitch, please," he imitated, throwing his hand. "And that punk muthafucka' Freddy, he played me! He used what he knew about me, against me, to get my girl. I thought he was my partner. Ain't no real stand-up dudes out here anymore, doc. Everybody's on the take. If it ain't your money they want, it's your woman. Then after that, it's your life. It's all fucked up out here. You don't know who to trust."

A moment of silence blanketed the room. Dex sat waiting for a conservative response from Dr. Barton. Dr. Barton didn't speak a word. He continued scratching on his pad. *Patient's anger and verbal hostility persists. Most of the issues emanate from past sexual encounters.*

He then looked to Dex over his glasses.

Dex held out his hands. "What you think, doc? What's your diagnosis on this?"

Dr. Barton crossed his legs, speaking with his pencil. "Well Dex, this particular incident you just described to me happened about eighteen years ago, correct?"

"True that."

"But yet, you speak strongly and aggressively about the situation as if it just recently occurred. From what you've told me, I would assume that you've disassociated yourself from Freddy years ago, right?"

Dex

"Of course, I have. I mean ... not really. Shit, I don't know. It's crazy, Doc. One minute Freddy's there in front of me talking, and then the next, I blacks out."

Dex began hitting his head with his palms. "I can't remember a damn thing at times. I keep telling myself I'm not crazy, but I just don't know what's wrong with me, doc?"

Dr. Barton could see Dex's frustration again building up. He could see the rage; that other side. He quickly changed the subject. "How has Coke been doing? Let's elaborate on him for a moment."

Dex hunched his shoulders. "What can I say about Coke? He's a good guy. He's never crossed me, bad-mouthed me, or done me wrong. He's a real friend. I'm now thirty-five, so that means, we've been buddies 'round thirty years now. It's like he's a part of me. He tells me personal things about him and I do the same with myself."

"You don't discuss our therapy sessions with Coke, do you?"

"Of course not," Dex lied. "Some things in your life you have to keep personal. If someone knows everything about you, then that person is subject to hurt you."

So true, the doctor silently agreed.

When the session was coming to an end, Dr. Barton handed Dex an overdue bill marked in red.

"Five thousand dollars?" looking to the doctor. "I'm that far behind?"

Dr. Barton moved in closer. "Dex, I like you. You're an alright guy," he said, patting Dex's hand. "Your life story is unfortunate, but at the same time, fascinating. You're one of my better patients, but your employer long ago discontinued your medical coverages. I have no choice but to suspend your treatments. Sorry, Dex. It's nothing personal, just business. You understand?"

The doctor then walked Dex out of his office into the receptionist lounge. "Dex, try to get at least half of that bill paid off. We can then resume our sessions. Sounds like a winner?" he smiled.

Dex gave no response. He instead turned away, not wanting to reveal the salty look on his face. *Ol' fat bastard, terminate my therapy sessions! I'll get you your money, somehow.*

Dr. Barton closed the door, taking offense to the silent treatment, yet he continued observing Dex through the peephole in the door.

Coke, seated in a lobby chair, overheard what the doctor had said. He was hardly disappointed by the news. He knew in therapy, his name was often the topic of discussion. Dex approached Coke, throwing the bill in his lap.

"Look at this bullshit!" he whispered in a rage. "Where am I gon' get that type of bread from? Tell me that! Where?"

He sat in the chair, crossing his legs, wagging his foot. He then stood again and began pacing the floor.

"Coke! What we gon' do, man? You know I ain't right wit' out my therapy. I ain't right."

Coke poked out his bottom lip in agreement. "I know this. You know this. The doc knows this. The question is, what are you gonna do about it?"

Dex stopped. "That's what the hell I'm asking you," looking at Coke as if he had the problem. "You got answers any other time. Come up with something now."

Coke said nothing because he had nothing to say. Dex's tantrum intensified.

Dex

What a nut, thought Dr. Barton, still eye-balling Dex through the peephole. The noise level soon caught the attention of Beverly, Dr. Barton's receptionist. She slid the locking glass window open.

"Dex!" she called, looking out into the lobby. "Dexter Chandler, is that you making all that fuss?"

"Huh?" he responded in a dimwitted manner.

"Yeah, it's you. Come here," she called making sure the slit between her breasts was exposed.

Dex walked over, immediately laying eyes on the oversized breasts. "Damn...," his lips expressed with no words. Beverly smiled.

"Just say the word Dexy Pooh, and big mama will let you rock her world," licking her top lip, blowing a kiss.

Dex sighed, "Shiiiddd... you mean that galaxy, right?" he joked. "I told you before, Beverly. I really don't get down with big girls like that. It's just, aahh..."

"What do you mean, aaahh...? My pussy gets wet just like any other woman you mess around with. Besides, big girls need love, too."

"Yeah, but I ain't the one who has to give it to them," Dex countered.

Beverly re-strategized, grabbing her breasts.

"Dex, you ain't never had a woman with titties this big and firm. I guarantee, when you stick your dick in-between these two beauties, and add some baby oil, you'll bust just like you were in some wet pussy."

Dex closed his eyes as he caught the chills. Beverly's visual conversation had him hot. Through his pants, he stroked the head of his penis. Coke, still seated in the chair, had seen and heard it all. He shook his head. *Freak.*

Nasty D!ck

Dr. Barton caught the evil eye behind the peephole. He didn't know what was being said, but from Dex's body language, it had to be about sex.

Dex leaned in closer to the receptionist's window. "So, Beverly. How did Dr. Barton get hold of that bill? I thought you and I had an agreement," he whispered.

"We did, but this morning Dr. Barton..."

"Ahem! Ahem!" went the doctor, making his presence known. "Beverly!" he pointed. "In my office!"

Beverly had the disappointing, *I just lost my job,* look on her face. Dr. Barton then looked to Dex.

"There aren't any more stand-up dudes left, you say? They're all on the take, correct? Well, it appears that you're one of them people you spoke of Dex. And about that bill you owe, don't worry about it. Just don't come back," he said, sliding the glass window shut.

Coke walked over, patting Dex's shoulder.

"Boy... I'll tell you. You and that dick done it again."

"Not right now, Coke. Not right now," Dex pleaded. "I just lost my doctor."

"Yes now, Dex! Right now!" Coke struck back. "Now that the good doctor is no longer in your ear, you might listen to me again for a change. Now, you might take in half the shit I've been trying to tell you. First of all, fuck Dr. Barton! Don't sshhh, me. Fuck him! I don't care if he hears me. You didn't need him from the start no way. I told you before, he's nothing himself but a big ass critical, conservative freak, with his fat ass; always fixin' his balls through his pants pocket. And don't think ol' Doc cut you off 'cause of the money you owe him. Nah, money is the least of his problems. It was over that receptionist, Beverly.

Dex

The good doctor has jungle fever. He's been fuckin' her and was afraid you were, too."

Dex shook his head like the thought disgusted him. Coke squint his eyes.

"Oh, don't act like you wasn't thinking about it. I've seen you with worse bitches than her. But don't get it twisted, Dex. I'm not here to judge you, scold you or embarrass you. I'm here to school you. You're my man of thirty years. I've had your back every since you were five years old. Have I not?"

"I guess," Dex nonchalantly hunched his shoulders. Coke felt the need to take him down memory lane.

"Ok, tell me this, when your father ran out on you and your mother years ago, who stood strong beside you? Who helped put meals on the table when you and she were strapped for cash?"

"You did," Dex agreed.

"Who took that golf club to your momma's boyfriend's head when he put his hands on her?"

"You did," he again answered, folding his arms, knowing there was more to come.

Coke went on to mention to Dex how he whipped Derrick, Leroy, and Binky's asses, one by one, plus all of the others that laughed at him the day he got hit by that car. Coke also boasted about how he located and took revenge on the driver of the car who'd hit him. Dex shook his head in pity.

"You didn't have to cut that boy up like you did. He just got scared after he hit me, that's all."

"Scared my ass!" Coke flung his hand. "That pink-skin muthafucka' ran you down like a dog, and then fled the scene. He killed you for all he knows. I gave him what he had coming. Don't come off on me weak like that, Dex."

Nasty D!ck

Dex had heard enough, ready to walk away.

Coke grabbed his arm. "Hold up Dex, man, I apologize. You know I sometimes come off aggressive, but I'm just trying to protect you, at the same time, make you a stronger man. I'm not trying to control you or tell you what to think, but I am telling you to think. Some of the decisions you've made on your own weren't the best of choices, like all them kids you have. What you got, seven, eight, or nine kids?"

"Seven!"

Might as well be nine, thought Coke. "With six different mothers', right?"

Dex was beginning to get an attitude. "You already know!"

"Yeah, I do, but I want you to understand my point, Dex. You're thirty-five years old with seven kids, six baby mommas', and you're broke with no plan. Now, most would view you as a man with his back against the wall. I don't. I see you as a man who's asking for some help and a little guidance. I understand not having your father in your life has been hard for you to deal with, but you don't need to spill your guts to some freak ass doctor. You can talk to me. I'll show you the way. I'll guide you through. Remember, there is no me without you. I'm here for you for life, Dex."

Coke then extended his hand.

Dex sighed. *I've been down this road with Coke before. This road leads to nothing but destruction. Coke is more relentless and crazier than anyone else I know. Yet he's so cool and laid back. It's hard to detect the monster he really is. I guess that's how most psychopaths really are. It's amazing to me how observant and knowledgeable Coke is about people and life. He reads everyone and everything like a book; like he's been here before or something. It's weird.*

Dex

Most times, he don't say a thing. He just sits back and watch. The shit is kind'a scary. But damn, I'm still in question about that statement he made. Am I really asking for help? Am I seeking guidance? Yeah, I guess I am. Shit, I have the gift of controlling these bitches and their pussies, but I can't control my own destiny. What kind of man am I?

After his thoughts, Dex reached out for Coke's hand. The two embraced for a hug.

"It's gon' be different this time, partner. I promise," Coke whispered into Dex's ear. "But first, you have to let go of that pain. Just let it go."

Dex understood. The two then exited Dr. Barton's office.

Nasty D!ck

The Truth Hurts

The buzzer sounded on the stove. Barbara reached inside the oven, pulling out her sweet potato pies. Like always, the pies were baked to perfection. She set them on the counter to cool. Dex had just walked into the house carrying a large paper bag, inhaling the sweet aroma.

"Mmmm, mmm... momma. That Thanksgiving food smells good, especially them pies," he remarked, sitting the bag on the table. "I could smell them through the front door. This is how I want my wife to cook on holidays when I get married."

Dex

Barbara laughed. "Married? Who? You?" She laughed again. "Boy, I don't think you're ever gon' be ready for that type of move. Marriage is a big responsibility. Don't get me wrong. You're a handsome young man, and I love my grandchildren. But, what woman in her right mind is gon' marry a man who already has seven children? She's going to know off the back, you can't keep it at home."

"Damn, momma, it's a good thing I can take a joke. And who says I can't keep it at home? I can be faithful, if I had the right woman," he added.

"The right woman? Dex, you wouldn't know her if she wore a sign around her neck. You're too busy watching for the butt, the breasts, and the thighs. You're not paying attention to all of the important stuff like, whether or not she can read or write. What is the relationship with her mother? Was her father in her life?"

Hmmm, that was an indirect statement, thought Dex, but he got the message.

Barbara continued. "You know son, the important things to know about a woman. Men today don't know how to measure a woman's worth. All y'all care about is how she sucked this, and how I bumped that. I be hearing y'all talk. You ignore the way a woman looks at you, how she treats you, and how she talks to you. How she finds everything about you beyond interesting. Y'all miss all of that. All you know is, 'bend it over baby, let me slap that a...'"

"Momma!"

"Well, it's true," Barbara shrugged her shoulders. "But I'm not one-sided on this topic. I know some of those females out there are a mess, too. It seems the young folks today are all out just to have a good time. They meet in one day, have sex and then go on to the next one. They're all in a rush. Half of them don't know how to love or know what it is to be in love."

Dex frowned. "Love! Ain't nobody got time for that," throwing his hand.

"Well, Dex, it would be nice if you'd brought a girl home to me that you thought you might be in love with. But its always been, ma', I met this girl and she's saying I got her pregnant," deepening her voice, imitating Dex.

Dex smiled. He then bust out laughing, knowing it was true. Barbara switched her conversation like the wind.

"And don't think I forgot about that day years ago when I walked in here on you, your uncle and that tramp. If I would've been a second later, ugh…!" she expressed at the thought of Dex having sex with Catwalk.

Dex quickly changed the subject, afraid his mother would again ask if or not he had sex with Catwalk that day. Barbara's sixth sense told her that he had, but for almost two decades straight, he denied it. He would never admit such a thing to his mother.

"Look, momma," said Dex, reaching inside the bag on the table. "I bought you your favorite holiday drink; a fifth of Hennessey!" placing the bottle on the counter. "See ma, your only son is thinking of you."

Barbara smiled. "Thinking of me? Thank you, son, but why don't you try thinking back to the day on the couch in there. I have good reasons for asking."

Dex blew out a breath, rolling his eyes. "Listen, momma, I done told you before. I didn't…"

Just then, the doorbell rang. Dex jumped at the opportunity to answer the door. He glanced through the peephole. He could see a white man standing on the porch; another gentleman off to the side.

Dex

Who are these muthafuckas? thinking, *The Police.*
"Who is it?" he asked, holding his ear to the door.
"Hi. It's Better Care. I have with me, patient: Emanuel Chandler here, for a home visit?"
"It's Uncle Manny, ma!"

Emanuel Chandler, AKA uncle Manny, was Barbara and Goose's older brother. In his day, Emanuel was intelligent, witty, handsome, charming, modest and humble with style. He was a book-smart guy with a lot of street sense; an uplifting type of person who people genuinely liked.

After attending the University of Michigan and earning his MBA, Emanuel landed himself a position at Greensboro Investment Group. There, he met Marla, a young graduate just out of college. Within six months, the two would be engaged. In another three, Marla would be pregnant.

Nothing was more important than family, to Emanuel. He loved to plan and organize all the family get-togethers. When the family was altogether in one place, he spoke to them about opening a family business. He talked about economic growth, investing, and saving for their futures.

He often flirted with the idea of them all living in one big house to subsidize the living expenses. The family was never too keen on that idea. They usually turned up their lips when the conversation surfaced.

One day after work, fifteen years ago, Manny expected to come home, kick off his shoes and rest. Instead, an armed, masked man met him inside his home. Manny threw his hands up, telling the intruder to take what he wanted. The presumed robber explained that he wasn't there for money. He said this was about his wife and the relationship she was having with Manny. It had been going on for over three years. Manny, thought by most to be straight and narrow, had several relationships outside his home, and couldn't narrow down exactly who the man's wife was.

He repeatedly apologized to the man, telling him it would never happen again. At that moment, an unexpected Marla burst through the front door, badly needing to urinate. This startled the gunman, who turned in her direction and fired his weapon. A single bullet struck her in the stomach. She collapsed to the floor.

This forced Manny to react. He screamed in anger as he rushed the masked man. The two fell to the floor as the gun, again, went off. When the smoke cleared, Manny laid shot in the head. His body twitched. He slowly lost consciousness. He felt himself dying. The room took on a sideways view as he lied with blood spilling from his head. The last thing he saw was a familiar face knelt down to him apologizing, yelling his name.

"Hi, Manny," greeted both Dex and Barbara at the front door. Manny didn't speak, he didn't smile, nor did he give Dex or Barbara any eye contact. He just silently walked into the house, sat in a chair, placed his hands in his lap and stared downward.

Dex and Barbara looked at one another, then to the care worker for answers. The care worker smiled.

"Emanuel gets that way sometimes, but don't you worry, that sailor will talk once he settles in; tends to speak his mind." The worker handed Barbara a folder. "In there is Emanuel's diet chart, list of rules for his safety, as well as your own, and... that's about it. Alrighty, you folks enjoy

Dex

your holiday evening. I'll be back to pick him up at nine." The care worker then waved good-bye, walking off the porch.

Dex closed the door. He and his mother turned to Manny, who appeared to be in a zombie-like state. Clearly, he wasn't the same free-spirited man he was years ago, no longer the strong link in the family chain.

Dex whispered, "Ma, what is it again uncle Manny has?"

"Brain damage," she whispered back. "The bullet that struck him in the head damaged parts of his brain."

Damn, thought Dex, only able to imagine the pain. "So, what you saying is, uncle Manny ain't right, right?"

"Yes and no. Manny's able to perform simple tasks by himself, with supervision. He can eat, exercise, go to the bathroom, even smoke a cigarette all by himself, but only under supervision. He can no longer comprehend how to pay bills, how to grocery shop, or how to simply mail off a letter. But Manny is gon' be alright. He's under lifetime care with Better Care, and they're good. I'm just glad my brother kept good insurance on himself."

At that moment Barbara was about to question Dex about his insurance coverage's, and also about his psyche treatments with Dr. Barton. But, the doorbell again saved him.

When the front door opened, Goose stepped in, along with his family, talking loud and proud. He looked, acted, and dressed the same as he did twenty years ago, as though he was stuck in time. His pump-waves style hairdo was even the same with the exception of the hairpiece on top.

Catwalk, Goose's wife of almost twenty years, was the second to enter. Now in her late forties, her breasts had more than doubled in size. She was thick in the waste and fat in the face. Her ass was so big, it looked unreal. She gave Dex a warm hug as she passed by, leaving behind a scent of cigarettes, perfume and spearmint gum. Dex was somewhat embarrassed with himself, knowing that she was the first woman he had ever fucked.

Third and last to enter the house was eighteen year old Donald Chandler, AKA Duck; the first and only child of Goose and Catwalk. In his short life, Duck had seen more sexual encounters than Magnum condoms. From the time he was three years old, he vaguely recalled his parents having sex next to him in bed, while he was thought to be asleep.

At five, peeking through a cracked bedroom door, he witnessed his first threesome. At the time, he didn't understand why his mother was sitting on another woman's face moaning, or why his father's face was between the same woman's legs, sticking out his tongue. It was puzzling.

By the age of thirteen, with ten years of eyeballing experience under his belt, young Duck had put his sexually advanced skills to the test. Equipped with dildos, clit feathers, anal beads, and blindfolds from home, he turned numerous young teen-aged females out. He was rocking worlds and fulfilling fantasies. But it wasn't until they felt his snake-like flickering tongue did he earn a real reputation. Like heroin addicts, they were all addicted, impatiently waiting and fiending for their next hit of Duck.

Duck stepped into the foyer. "What's up, cuzzo?" shaking Dex's hand.

"You, cousin," responded Dex, closing the door. He then looked Duck over. The two shared strong characteristics. *Wow! Duck looks a lot like me,* he thought, calculating the years from that day on the couch with

Dex

Catwalk, now understanding why his mother was so persistent with her questions. He shook it off.

"So, Duck, what has it been, seven, eight, nine years since I last saw you?"

"Naw cuz. It's been ten years. I was eight years old the last time I was up here. You just had your first kid. Remember?"

"You're right. Time be flyin'," thinking how he'd fathered six more children since then.

By this time, Barbara and Catwalk were in the dining room greeting each other with fake hugs and kisses. It had been ten years since the two women had seen one another, but if another ten years had went by without the pair seeing each other, neither woman would shed a tear.

Goose, standing in the kitchen, almost came to tears, looking at his older and only brother, Manny. He hadn't seen Manny since his near death experience fifteen years ago. Before then, he couldn't remember a thing but the good times. Goose suddenly went back in time, thinking back fifteen years ago to the last family get-together Manny had planned.

"Man, you sure do pick the best days for family get-togethers," said Goose to Manny, grabbing a cold beer from the cooler. "And gimme one those burgers, they look damn good."

Manny, working the grill, handed Goose a burger. "You see, lil bro, this is what it's all about. Family, sharing and giving to those that count. Look," he pointed with the spatula in hand to the elders sitting in the lawn chairs. "You got Aunt Betty, Aunt Nell, Francine, Lorraine, and Blanche. Even Ms. Diane is here. We've known her most of our lives." Goose nodded, having a little history with Ms. Diane.

Nasty D!ck

"Over there," Manny directed to the card table. "You got Uncle Kenny, Charles, Oscar, and Otha. Uncle Otha is sick with cancer, you know?" Goose took a swig of his beer, already aware. "It ain't everyday we get to see them like when we were youngsters, bro. How much more time do they have left on this earth?" Goose had no answer. "Then look at the kids Goose, the kids. They're the replacements of old life. The kids are growing up so fast."

The two focused their attention on twenty-year old Dex, with his boyish, manly traits. Then on to three-year old Duck who was playing with the other children.

"And there's my bundle of joy," pointed Manny, to a pregnant Marla, who appeared to be feasting for two. "Doctor says it's a boy."

Goose hugged his brother, slapping his shoulder.

"A boy! Congratulations, man! Looks like our two sons will be growing up together."

Manny gave a dry smile. "Yeah..."

"Damn Manny, I be traveling with the dance group so much, focusing on myself, I never took the time to see the family values you've pointed out to me today. How could I have been so selfish? I've missed out on a lot of good years. This life is so much greater than myself," looking to Duck whom was running past. Goose grabbed him by the arm and picked him up. He kissed Duck's cheeks, hugged him and set him free. He then strolled over to Catwalk, planting on her a deep, hard, kiss. Catwalk was shocked. It had been a long time since Goose kissed her that way. She could tell something or someone had gotten to him, eyeing Manny.

Just then, Goose turned to Manny, who was still on the grill. He held up five fingers, pointing towards the house.

Meet you in five minutes? In the house? Okay, Manny confirmed, holding up his spatula. He then went back to flipping the meat, shaking his head. *I think my brother done saw the light a little too late.*

Within fifteen minutes, Manny tossed his apron and entered the house through the patio door. He had no idea of what his brother wanted. He figured it was to again thank him for helping him to see the light. He knew his brother's thoughts on family values were often shallow.

Inside the house, Goose was nowhere in sight. Manny checked the front room, the living room, upstairs and the basement with no luck. *Now, I know I saw him walk in the house,* scratching his head. He then walked back to the patio door and looked throughout the back yard. He could see Duck still playing, so he knew Goose had to be around.

Right then, Manny saw Uncle Otha out the corner of his eye, with his cane in his hand, struggling to climb the basement stairs. Manny rushed to his aid.

"Uncle Otha! Why were you in the basement?"

"'Cause I had to piss!" he spat. "That damn Goose is hogging the bathroom up here!"

Manny apologized, assisting Uncle Otha back outside. Afterwards, he headed to the bathroom and aggressively beat on the door.

"Goose!" he called. "Goose, are you in there?"

"C'mon in," Goose answered in a laid back tone.

Manny entered the long, narrow bathroom, covering his nose, expecting to find Goose on the toilet with a bad case of the shits. Instead, hoards of steam rushed from the hot shower, into his face. He couldn't see or hear a damn thing. The heavy water beating against the shower curtain drowned out any sounds. Slowly, he inched closer. Just then, Slap! Slap!

"Yeah, bitch, ride that dick for daddy!" harmonized Goose, striking the sides of the woman's ass.

Nasty D!ck

As Manny's eyes came into focus, he couldn't believe it. *Goose is fucking in my bathroom at our family get-together?* He was somewhat disappointed, but the erection in his pants said otherwise. Even though conservative in his profession, and a short time away from being a family man, Manny liked pussy, too. His hot, sweaty face told him to get the hell out of that bathroom, but his planted feet just wouldn't seem to move. He stood by and watched as the woman in a backward motion, grip the edge of the bathtub and in slow motion, stroke her body up and down on the head of Goose's dick who was positioned on the toilet.

Goose watched from behind as her pussy lips retracted back and forth off of him, loving the feeling. He then looked to his brother, smiling and pointing as if to say, *You're next.* Manny began catching the shakes as he pictured himself fucking in the same position. *Mmph!*

He could tell the way Goose's body was pulling, the woman was locking her vaginal lips. Suddenly, she loosened her pussy and dropped all the way down to the nuts. Goose's head fell backward onto the toilet tank cover. Manny's toes cringed with ecstasy, almost choking on the saliva built up in his mouth.

Damn, she's a pro, he thought, catching his breath. He was still unable to make out the woman's identity, whose face was hung over the bathtub full of steam. At this point, it didn't matter who the woman was. Manny's dick was throbbing hard. The pressure was on and he needed relief. Any morals of being a committed fiancé were out the window. He unzipped his pants.

Goose looked. "Yeah, bro, that's what I'm talking about. C'mon and get you some of this. This is for you, for helping me. Lift on up, baby. Manny's ready," he told the woman as she stood up and her face came into view.

"Catwalk?" Manny questioned.

"Of course," she replied, "Who else did you expect?" walking over to Manny. "Goose knows better than to bring another bitch around this family."

Catwalk stood neck length to Manny, staring upward into his brown eyes. She then took a squatting position down to her knees. She gently caressed Manny's balls, kissed the head of his dick, palmed his ass and took him into her mouth. Catwalk gave him two deep throat headshots as an appetizing tease.

Next, she stood up, grabbed his dick, rubbed it between the warm crack of her ass and jumped in the shower. Manny almost passed out. He grew weak in the knees. One more stroke of head and he would've came all over her ass. Manny gave his brother a look of, *Damn, she's a bad muthafucka!* Goose, leaning against the face bowl, smiled like, *I know. That's my wife. Get her,* nodding his head.

Manny turned back to Catwalk. She was bent over in the shower, letting the steamy water drip from her pussy. Several times, she ran her finger across her clit, tasting herself.

With two fingers, she separated her vaginal lips, displaying her pink insides, giving Manny a non-blinking hard stare. It was a clear invitation to fuck. That was it. Manny was ready. His hard dick was in his hand. There was no stopping him now. But first, he felt the need to urinate to drain himself of any existing semen. He didn't want to risk getting Catwalk pregnant.

Just as he stood over the toilet, Whap! Whap! Whap! "Uhh…uhh…uh," sounded Catwalk, passionately.

Nasty D!ck

From the sound of the wet clashing bodies, Manny didn't bother to turn around. He simply wiped the medicine cabinet mirror next to him. He could see Goose in the shower with Catwalk, popping beads of water from her ass every time he thrust. *Look at this ol' selfish bastard,* thought Manny.

To ensure herself a deeper and harder fuck, Catwalk used her hands to spread both her ass cheeks. Goose was deep inside of her. Suddenly, there was a knock at the door.

"Manny!" Marla called. "Are you okay? You've been in there for quite a while."

The trio froze like mannequins. *Oh shit!* They didn't know what to do. Goose fiercely waved his hand to Manny, suggesting, *Tell her something!*

Manny stuttered, "Uhh... y-yeah, I'm fine sweetie. B-be out in a minute." He then pulled up his pants, fixed his clothes and slowly exited the bathroom, upset that he didn't get a chance to fuck.

Goose came out of the thought, smiling about that memorable day. It made him want to give his brother a hug, but he couldn't bring himself to do so. To see Manny in this condition was too painful. In a fucked up way, Goose wished his brother would have just died.

Then suddenly, Manny stared Goose down with evil eyes, almost as if he sensed his thoughts. A below-zero chill shot down Goose's spine. Then slowly, he backed away and exited the kitchen.

By this time, Dex and Duck had retired to the den. The two were reminiscing, going over old photos.

Ducked laughed. "Look at this shit, here cuz. What were you thinking about?" he asked Dex. "High ass shorts,

Dex

tight ass clothes. Y'all gear was whack as hell back in the day."

Dex grabbed the picture. "Oh yeah, this was 1989. I had on my Pistons jersey shorts. They had won the championship that year. Boy, back then, this was the shit!" he claimed.

Duck twisted his lips, "Whatever," thinking, *Not anymore.* Duck continued to surf the photo album. Just then, he waved Dex in closer. "Look, check this out. Here's a picture of me, Catwalk, and Goose," referring to his parents by their names. "I had to be about four or five years old on this picture."

Dex scanned the photo, focusing on Duck. He then grabbed a childhood photo of himself, comparing the two. There was no doubt, the resemblance was there. *Duck actually might be my son.* Dex showed the two pictures to Duck and asked, "What you think?"

"'Bout what?" replied Duck.

"These pictures. You and I look a lot alike, don't you think?"

Duck glanced over the photos, not yet answering. Instead, he flipped back through the photo album. He stopped at an old picture and pulled it out, pointing, "Who does the two boys' right here look like to you, Dex?"

Dex set all three photos side-by-side, giving a magnifying stare. He smirked.

"They look like you and me," he answered.

"Exactly. And do you know who those two boys are?"

"Of course, I do. That's Goose and Manny."

"Right again, big cuz. We all look alike down to the women in the family, strong genes. Anyway, Goose got the same picture in his photo album back home."

Nasty D!ck

Right then, Dex let go of any thoughts or possibilities of Duck being his son. *Besides, I've got enough kids to worry about, anyway.*

Soon, the conversation between Dex and Duck turned personal. Dex was the first to share some of his personal feelings. He told Duck about how he felt by his father not being in his life. He spoke about how he hadn't seen his dad since the age of five, and how his father went to work one day and never came back home. Dex said his father's thirty-year absence wouldn't have been so bad if he would have at least called him on holidays.

Dex failed to mention his counseling sessions with Dr. Barton or the fact that he was on medications. He felt that would be disclosing too much information. He did, however, mention Coke and the guidance role he plays in his life. Dex said if it weren't for Coke, he'd probably be dead.

Afterwards, Duck went on to explain his life situations that bothered him. He began by telling Dex about the strong and close relationship he and his mother shared. He told Dex that Catwalk was a misunderstood person by the family. He admitted that his mother was once a sexually charged person, but he explained that most of the sexual acts that she'd committed with other parties were on the word of Goose. "Even the encounter on the couch with you and Catwalk years ago was a setup by him."

A white, pale look pasted over Dex's face. Duck smiled. "You didn't think I knew about that, huh? But I ain't trippin'. That was before me. And just to clear up the air, Dex, you're not my father. Goose is."

Dex felt both relief and disappointment, and a little embarrassed that Duck knew the truth. Duck continued his story with claims that Goose orchestrated all the ménage à trois and orgies his mother took part in. He also told of how

Dex

one day, his father verbally scorned Catwalk for not wanting to have sex with three strange men at a swinger's party. When she pleaded her case of being tired and weary, the verbal abuse intensified.

"Goose is my daddy and I love him Dex, but flat out, that muthafucka' is a dog. And still, after all that fuckin' and fightin' my parents done been through, Catwalk still loves Goose's dirty ass drawers."

"Damn," said Dex. "Sounds like unc is off the chain but you know what, Duck? That's Catwalk and Goose's life. I wanna know what's up with you. What's going on in Duck's world?"

Again, Duck smiled. "Shiiid… what you think is goin' on? I'm nineteen. I'm fuckin' all day, everyday."

Dex looked in disbelief. "Fuckin' all day? You probably ain't doin' nothing but navel poking."

"Naw, big cuz. Let me break it down to you how I regulates these females.

I was born a freak, saw it at three
Goose and Catwalk in the bed, fuckin' right next to me
By the time I was thirteen, I ran with the game
Puttin' dick in them girls, beating pussies out the frame
I'm nineteen now, a grown ass man
Adolescent years behind me, sexual skills advanced
You got a dry ass pussy? Won't get wet?
Yo' man ain't fuckin' you right? Give you bold ass sex?
Well come and see Duck, I'll lay you out right
I'll tear that ass down, put some dick in your life
Let's fuck on the flo', let's fuck in the bed
I'll be fuckin' yo' face, while you giving me head
I'll be up in you deep, I'll be up in you far
I'll be up in you naked, I'll be up in you raw

Nasty D!ck

Are you scared? You shy?
Don't talk to you like that?
Well check this out girl, I'll run my tongue in yo' crack
Let me tease that puss with this wide ass tongue
Leave you shaking and quivering after you cum
You see what I'm saying? That brought you a smile
You wanna get loose, c'mon baby get wild
I ain't just talkin' shit, I can back it up
You'll be screaming Duck, while you're bussin' your nuts
Let a freak in your life, let a freak in your world
Let me chauffeur that ass, take control of you girl
Bust once, bust twice, bust three straight times
Bust so many times, tears will come to your eyes
You'll value me, cherish me, hold my name close
'Cause when it comes to the sex, you already know
I'm tellin' you cousin, young Duck be fuckin'
And I was only jokin', I be using my rubbers
But not at all times, that would be telling a lie
Fuckin' raw ass pussy should be a sexual crime
"You're right," said Dex, "Keep a glove on your shit.
How do you think I ended up with seven muthafuckin' kids."

At that point, Dex and Duck broke into laughter.
Later on, family members and guests began to arrive for the
Thanksgiving dinner. The house quickly began to fill. There
were twenty to thirty people throughout the house. It wasn't
long before the den was invaded, which forced Dex and
Duck to mingle.
"Hey..."
"How you doin', baby?"
"My, you've grown."

Dex

"Ain't seen you in a long time," greeted the family and friends, exchanging hugs, kisses, back rubs, and handshakes.

Goose was in the living room entertaining his elder uncles with some old stories and dance steps. Catwalk was seated in the dining room, telling the younger women how fine she once was. Barbara was in the kitchen putting the finishing touches on the meal and talking with her cousin, Tanya, at the same time, she put away her bottle of liquor. She knew that the more people drank, the longer they stayed.

Everyone in the house was talking and laughing, catching up on old times. Even Manny was making his way around the residence. Family and friends greeted and shook hands with him, but he was unable to remember a soul. However, he did keep eye-balling Catwalk from the kitchen. A faint memory of her face kept coming into play. Catwalk caught Manny a couple of times looking her way but when she looked in his direction, he would turn his head.

Suddenly, "Barbara!" shouted Goose, heading toward the kitchen. "Barbara, where's that Hennessey? I need a drank! I know you got some stashed around here."

As Goose entered the kitchen, Manny again gave him that evil look. Goose had forgotten his brother was in the kitchen, now trying to hold his composure the best he could. He started stuttering.

"H-h-hey, cousin Tanya," he said, waving before turning to his sister. "Umm... Barbara, umm..."

Goose began rubbing his neck. He could feel Manny's cold eyes behind him, starring. He could picture his brother so clear; the aging wrinkles on his forehead, the permanent creases in his cheeks, and that mean squinting right eyebrow, which spoke, *You dirty muthafucka!*

Nasty D!ck

Goose started snapping his fingers, unable to remember why he'd came into the kitchen.

"What's the matter with you?" asked a frowning Barbara. "You said you need a drink, remember? It's right there next to you on the counter," she pointed, handing him a glass.

Goose tried to pour himself a drink but his hand was shaky and jittery. More liquor landed on the counter then in his glass.

"Jesus Goose," said Barbara. "That's good liquor you're spilling." She yanked the bottle from his hand and poured him a drink. Like a madman, Goose downed the entire drink. He then slowly peered over his shoulder, but to his surprise, Manny was gone.

Barbara whispered to him. "Goose, I don't know what has gotten into you, but you have to pull yourself together." She then exited the kitchen carrying the dressing and cranberry sauce, followed by cousin Tanya with the macaroni and cheese.

Shortly thereafter, everyone joined hands around the dining room table and bowed their heads in prayer to bless the food. Dex did the honors.

"Dear Heavenly Father, we give thanks to Thee for allowing us another day to awake. We give our thanks for allowing us this here day to nourish our souls. We again give thanks for allowing each and every person to arrive here safely today and please, allow their journey home to be a safe one as well. Amen."

"Amen," everyone chimed in unison.

The cherry wood dining room table only seated six but that didn't matter, the hungry stomachs found a way. Guests were in every part of the house eating from their

Dex

plates. They stood in the kitchen, sat in the living room, the den, on the steps leading to the upstairs, wherever a seat was available. Dex and Duck found their way down into the finished basement with a few others.

"God damn!" expressed Duck, dousing his biscuit in turkey gravy. "This food is on point. Catwalk don't be makin' no shit like this on holidays."

"Shiiiid, man, I grew up on these types of meals almost everyday," said Dex as he set his empty plate aside. "Why do you think I ain't left home yet? For example, look over there," Dex pointed across the basement. "That's my second oldest son and his mother. She's the McDonald-est eating bitch in the world. Broad can't cook a lick. She can't even make Kool-Aid. I'll go over their house and it don't be shit in the refrigerator," he said, shaking his head. "These women nowadays do not cook."

Right then, Dex's son's mother, Cree, walked over to where Dex was seated. After introducing herself to Duck, she looked to Dex.

"Dex, when I leave from here, which will be shortly, I'm going out with my girls tonight and getting drunk. Are you coming over later?"

"Hell yeah," answered Dex with no hesitation. "I'll be there, no doubt." Dex and Duck then watched as Cree walked back to her seat.

Duck smiled, shaking his head. "No disrespect, big cuz, but she ain't nev'a gotta cook. That girl has a nice fat ass on her."

"She sure does," co-signed Dex. "And she got the k-splash...! Pussy stays wet. It be so wet sometimes, I can't even fuck it. I might get ten strokes in, then I gotta pull out or I'll bust."

Nasty D!ck

"Whew!" smiled Duck, eyeing Cree. "I'll buy that for a dollar."

After the second servings of food went around, the cards, game boards, cigarettes and liquor came into play. Dex, Goose, Duck and Uncle Kenny took over the dining room table with dominoes. Catwalk got together with a few of the young ladies to play spades in the den. Another group decided to play Keno in the basement, while Barbara, her cousin and a couple of friends played Bid Whist in the living room.

Manny came up with his own game. He sat behind Barbara camouflaging himself watching Catwalk from afar. Her face, her eyes and her lips were familiar to him, but he couldn't quite place them. Just then, he closed his eyes. Scenes from the day he was shot begin to ravage his mind.

"We can work this out! What's your wife's name?" he envisioned himself saying.

"You know my wife's name, muthafucka!" screamed the man holding the gun. "You've been fuckin' her since day one!"

"Okay, just take it easy, bro…"

"Oohhh… Manny! I've been shot!" screamed Marla. Bbbooooommm!!

Manny jumped, opening his eyes, snapping out of his trance, scanning the room.

Goose was leaning back in the chair looking to the living room, watching Manny as he came to. *Ol' crazy bastard should've died.*

"C'mon, Unc, your play," said Dex, growing impatient.

Dex

"Oh, excuse the hell out of me. Domino, muthafucka!" yelled Goose as he slapped the game-winning piece down onto the table.

"Goose, please! Your mouth!" hollered Catwalk from the den.

Full of liquor and hot-tempered, Goose struck back.

"You watch your damn mouth, Cat! Shit! Leave me the hell alone and worry about your damn self. I'm in here doin' my thang," he spoke, irritated.

Catwalk was disturbed by Goose's loud tone. She felt fronted off. "Yeah, okay Goose, keep doin' your thang."

"Yeah, I am!" he fired back. "Been doin' it and gon' keep on doin' it! I don't need yo' ass!"

Catwalk heard Goose's last statement, but she left it alone. Folks sitting around the game and card tables could tell the beef was personal. They had no intentions of interfering. They knew that intervening in an argument between a husband and his wife most times would mean trouble for themselves.

Dex began to scramble the dominoes for a new game. After the players took their share of the game pieces, Goose made the first play.

"Give me ten!" he again shouted, slapping the spotted-white tile onto the table.

Uncle Kenny then took his turn. It was now on Duck, who was still bothered by his parents' argument. He got up from the table and walked out the front door. Dex followed to make sure he was alright.

At that point, Goose grew angrier, letting it all go. "You see there, bitch! Your big ass mouth done wrecked the game! You get on my fuckin' nerves!"

"Alright now, Goose!" said Barbara from the living room. "That will be enough!"

47

But it was too late. Catwalk was already on her way from the den. Her heavy footsteps could be heard pounding the floor.

"What did you say?" she barked. "What did you call me? A bitch?" now in Goose's face.

Goose relaxed, now that he had Catwalk's undivided attention. His cigarette was pinned between his lips, off to the side. He puffed it a couple of times, blowing out three smoke rings.

"Did I call you a bitch?" he replied, as he stared Catwalk in the eye. "I'm sorry. I meant to say *fat* bitch!"

The room stood still. Jaws dropped and mouths hung open.

"Oh, my God...," some whispered.

"Did you hear what Goose just said?"

"That's their business. Let them handle that," said others."

This wasn't the first or the hundredth time that Goose had called Catwalk a bitch. She could handle the name-calling. What she didn't like is that it was being said on Thanksgiving and in front of his family.

"So, you're just gonna disrespect me like this, in front of your family?"

Goose took a sip from his drink.

"What does it matter, Cat? My family ain't never liked you, no way. Besides, whores get no respect."

"Eeewww..., family or not, Goose is wrong for that."

"He's drunk. He don't know what he's sayin'."

"If that was my husband, I would beat his ass."

Family and friends were shocked by the degrading comments. Stunned most of all was Catwalk. She took two steps back, holding her chest but Goose wasn't finished yet. He reached inside the sleeve of his coat hanging on the back

Dex

of his chair. He then flung a set of stapled papers over to his wife. She picked up the papers, reading the bold print.

"File for divorce?" she read indisbelief. "Goose, you're divorcing me?"

"You just read it, didn't you?"

Catwalk's face turned blank. Whatever love she'd had for Goose over the years died right there. With all of her might, she reached back and slapped the shit out of Goose. Whap!

His slim, tall frame flipped out of the chair to the floor. The people in the basement came running up the stairs to see what the commotion was. Goose lay dazed. The heavy-handed blow had caught him completely off guard. Catwalk stood over him, unleashing her fury.

"Muthafucka! I gave you twenty years of my life and this is what you give me in return? A fuckin' divorce?" tossing the papers at him. "Hell, naw Goose! I might be a bitch at times, but what woman ain't? And then you fix your mouth to call me a whore? A whore, Goose? Who died and made you king of character? True, I done did some shit I ain't proud of, but if it made you happy, I did it. We did it together. It's no secret. Everybody knows about our past swinging life, even our son. So, how can *you* of all people, judge me now? I was your wife, Goose. I was only what you wanted me to be. But, fuck it. If we gon' tell some shit, we might as well tell it all."

Goose finally stood, with some assistance from a relative. He sat back down in his chair. His hairpiece was sideways on top of his head. He then tried to reason with Catwalk.

"Okay baby, calm down. We can finish this discussion at home," he said, while trying to straighten out his hairpiece. Catwalk ignored him.

Nasty D!ck

"Tell them, Goose. Tell them about the big Mack, Playa' you supposed to have been, 'cause the women here in your family appeared to be fooled by you. They don't know that you're a jealous ass punk, do they? Let me tell y'all. Goose would put together these orgies and freak parties and would beg me to participate. So, when I did join in and started enjoying myself, this damn fool would get mad. Why do you think him and uncle Otha fell out years ago?"

Mouths again dropped.

"Uncle Otha? Uncle Otha?" some uttered in disbelief, looking to his direction.

Uncle Otha simply turned his head.

Catwalk continued. "Mmm... mmph! Goose done had me all in the family. It's a couple of faces I see hear today that he had me get down with years ago."

Some of the men who were there with their wives began covering up their faces. Out of anger, Catwalk pointed out one of the men, who was cocky enough not to cover his face. His wife gave him that look. Catwalk then spoke of the sexual encounter with Dex, which infuriated Barbara, but confirmed her suspicions.

"Oh, you ain't got nothing to be mad about, Barbara," said Catwalk. "Your name was almost in this, too. For years, Goose had been trying to figure a way to get you in bed with us."

Barbara covered her face in shame. Goose did the same. *I'ma kill this bitch!* he thought. There was nothing that anyone could say. A terrible dark secret was brought out into the light. The awful truth was bleeding ears.

"Alright, that's enough from you, Katrina!" defended cousin Tanya. "You're embarrassing our family."

Catwalk hunched her shoulders.

50

Dex

"What do I care about embarrassing your family? Like Goose said, y'all ain't never liked me no way. Anyway, sit yo' ass down, Tanya! Goose done told me all about you. Don't let me have to put your shit out in the street."

Tanya left the room.

Just then, Dex and Duck returned, hoping things had calmed down, but from the tight looks on faces in the room, they knew things hadn't.

With her finger pointed less than an inch from Goose's nose, Catwalk proclaimed, "I was in love with this man and he tricked me into thinking he was in love with me, too. But you see what that got me, right? Some *divorce* papers," she laughed. *Ol' muthafucka'.*

"I did love you, Cat. I really did," insisted Goose.

Catwalk shook her head.

"No, you didn't Goose. You never have. But there was one man who did love me; who wanted to be with me; a man who is actually my son's biological father."

"I knew it!" said Barbara. "Gon' and tell 'em who Duck's daddy really is," as she looked to Dex.

Necks snapped. Eyes bucked. Whispers again engulfed the house.

"Biological father?"

"Goose ain't Duck's daddy?"

"You know she's a whore," the family spoke.

Goose stood. "What the hell you talkin' 'bout Cat? Duck ain't got no other daddy but me!"

Dex suddenly emerged, pushing his way into the dining room. "Catwalk, you don't have to put your business out there like that. Duck already explained it to me. I know I'm not his father. Goose is."

Nasty D!ck

Catwalk pointed to Goose. "That bitch there ain't Duck's daddy! And neither are you, Dex. Duck is *Manny's* child."

"Manny!" Surprised, everyone shifted their eyes to Manny, who was in the living room still sitting in the chair, staring back.

Catwalk explained. "Manny and I got together the first week I met Goose. He always pledged his love for me, but like a dummy, I stayed with the man I loved. Our quiet relationship continued for three years until one day, Goose saw Manny leaving the house. I told Goose he only came over to see Duck, but I could see the doubt in his eyes. Then a couple of days later, Goose came running in the house with blood all over him, saying, *I fucked up.* Thirty minutes later, I heard Manny and Marla had been shot."

Everyone's eyes and attention had now shifted to Goose, who was giving Catwalk a heated stare, as if to say, *You bitch!* But at that moment, he burst into tears. The nightmare which had haunted him for fifteen years was finally out in the open.

In tears herself, Barbara slapped Goose's face over and over again. "You shot our brother, Goose? How could you shoot our brother?" she cried.

Dex and Duck couldn't hold back their tears. With the exception of Catwalk, there wasn't a dry eye in the house. She had no tears, especially for a family who never gave a damn about her. She could care less. However, she did look to Manny and wondered what could have been years ago.

Right then, Manny's eye caught something. He began looking high and low trying to see into the living room past people walking back and forth. He got up from his seat to take a closer look. He could see Goose's weeping face lying on the cherry wood table. Manny then turned his head sideways, picturing the familiar weeping face from years ago. As Goose raised up to wipe his tears, he noticed his brother standing in front of him.

"Pow!" said Manny. "Pow! Pow! Pow!" he repeated, pointing his hand in a pistol fashion in Goose's face.

Goose could only bring himself to hug his brother and plead for his forgiveness. He then retired to the basement, away from all of the accusing stares.

Soon, Catwalk, Duck, and the other visitors were gone. Manny and his caregiver was the last to leave.

After putting up the food, Dex and Barbara were ready to turn in for the night.

"Ma, you know Goose is still down in the basement. Is there anything you wanna say to him before we go to bed?"

With tears in her eyes, Barbara shook her head, *No.* "It's going to be a long time before I forgive Goose for what he done to Manny but make sure you set some blankets by the stairs. He'll get them." The two then retired for the night.

After tossing and turning for about four or five hours, Dex got out of bed. He walked down to the kitchen for a drink. He poured himself a glass of orange juice, thinking about some of the things Catwalk had said about Goose.

"Whew," shaking his head. *How is unc gon' come back from this one? And that thing about Manny?* That's fucked up."

Just then, Dex noticed the blankets he set out for Goose were gone. *Let me check on him,* he thought as he crept into the dark basement. He didn't want to disturb his uncle's sleep by turning on the lights, so he slowly made his way over to the couch where his uncle was thought to be asleep, feeling around. But to his surprise, Goose wasn't there.

Right then, Dex observed a silhouette figure from across the room. What he saw was disturbing. He took a hard swallow, closing his eyes, hoping what he saw wasn't real. Dex turned on the lights. Goose was dead, slowly twirling, hanging by the neck from a support beam in the basement.

Dex

The Agency

"Aahhrrr…," roared Freddy as he pulled the woman's panties off with his teeth.

She giggled. "Eeeww, a carnivorous freak."

Freddy then blindfolded the butt-naked woman tying her hands to her ankles. He now had complete control. He took position behind the flickering light of the candles, staring at her nude body across the bed. Her legs were cocked wide open. *Nothing but pussy,* he exhaled, admiring the scene, now eye-balling Ché's other grand features; her large, d-cup breasts that stood firm; her smooth, round, mammoth-like ass in-which he loved to slap, and her v-shaped frame, which held it all together. Extraordinary was an understatement.

"Damn Ché, you a bad muthafucka', said Freddy."

"How bad?"

"Super bad…"

"Oh really? That's what you tell me, but why don't you come and show me."

Freddy was honored by the request. He opened his robe and flung it from his back like a bullfighter. Ché lay tingling with anticipation. Even though blindfolded, she could still picture Freddy's lean, muscular physique, his

Nasty D!ck

strong ballpoint shoulders, his deep chiseled abs, his athletic thighs, and his tight ass. The thought made her drench.

Freddy snatched Ché by her restraints, sliding her body to the edge of the bed, positioning her onto her back. She loved how Freddy took control. He then palmed her lightly-shaven vagina.

"What's all that? What's all that, huh?" he asked.

"You know what it is. That's my fat pussy," she spoke in a devilish tone.

"Fat pussy, huh?"

Freddy dropped to his knees. He began stroking her vagina with his nose and his face, then with his tongue.

Ché bit her lip, trying to hold back her cries of passion but it was useless. Freddy was that good. He gently pinned her clitoris between his top and bottom lip, sucking and licking it with his tongue. First side to side, then up and down, finally in circular motions. Ché tried to resist. She tried to run, but when you're tied up like cattle meat, there's nowhere to run to. She lied still, continuing to take the tongue-lashing, loving it.

Freddy finally came up for some air. His face was soaking wet. He dried it with a towel and looked back to Ché. She was still catching the shakes from the multiple orgasms she had.

"I need some water, baby," she requested.

"No problem. I got you."

Freddy fetched Ché some water from the kitchen. Still in restraints, he sat her up for a drink. But instead of putting the glass to her lips, he dipped his dick inside the glass and let her suck the water off of it, until the glass was nearly empty. Next, Freddy rubbed his dick around her face, jaw and lips. Ché was loving it, unable to get enough. Being blindfolded made it that much more exciting.

Dex

"You love my dick?" asked Freddy, guiding it in and out of her mouth.

"I love your dick," she answered, licking the head. "I would love it even more if you fucked me with it."

That's all Freddy needed to hear. He untied her and flipped her onto all fours in one motion. She was face down and ass up. Freddy was just inserting his dick when, Click! The television was turned off. Startled, Freddy turned around.

"Damn, Coke, you scared me. How did you get in here?"

"Fuck how I got in here. Didn't I tell you to get rid of that video? What kind of man watches the same footage of himself fucking over and over everyday?"

"It's a classic," Freddy insisted.

"Classic, my ass, Freddy. You're 'bout bad as Dex," he said as he ejected the DVD, sliding it into his pocket. "If your wife was to catch a glimpse of this, she would sic the dogs on your ass. It'll be over with."

"It might be over with anyway," Freddy mumbled, turning his head.

Coke was bothered. "What do you mean?" he asked.

"I meant just what I said. It might be over with. Ahbicdee (Uh-biss´-uh-dee) is trippin'."

"She's trippin'? About what? What did you do?"

Freddy sat for a minute thinking. He was trying to figure out a way to candy-coat the truth, but the hard truth was the only way.

Coke folded his arms. "C'mon, muthafucka! Let's hear it," he demanded.

Freddy began to tell Coke of how he tried to pull a side deal without him. He explained how Ocknock, their mutual business associate, had placed a rush order for a

Nasty D!ck

Caucasian girl, no older than three years old, with blond hair and blue eyes. Instead of Freddy contacting Coke and the two of them strategizing the abduction plan together as usual, Freddy went solo with the job.

He told Coke that within an hour, he'd found the perfect match in comparison to the picture that was given to him to fill the order. He then claimed to have taken his victim, a little girl, from a day care playground in Warren, Michigan.

Coke and Freddy were involved in an international child-smuggling ring, which passed itself off as an adoption agency stationed in South America. Couples from around the world, who have had unfortunate miscarriages, unsuccessful artificial inseminations and/or have tried numerous times over the years to have children, were their biggest clients.

After surfing hundreds of photos provided by the agency, clients would pay anywhere from $75,000 to $150,000 per child depending on how old the child was and from what part of the world the child was being ordered from. A child could range from as young as newborn to three years old. Any older and it would be difficult to successfully brainwash them.

Ocknock, a medical doctor from Nigeria, and one of twelve illegal adoption agents stationed in the U.S., settled grounds in Detroit to branch his operation. There, he met Freddy, who introduced him to Coke. Under Ocknock's eye, the two received child abduction training. They were taught how to observe an easy target, when and where to strike, and how to spot and avoid detection cameras. After two months of training, the kidnapping duo displaced ten children from their homes, placing them in new ones around the world.

Dex

Freddy continued. "So, I get the girl to Ocknock's lab, right? But even before he runs her blood tests, he tells me the girl is no good, she's sick and to take her back to where I found her."

Coke listened, shaking his head.

"I said, 'Ocknock, it's daylight. What do I look like taking a kidnapped white girl back to where I kidnapped her from in the middle of the day? That's asking to be locked up."

"So, what did Ock say?"

"He didn't say shit. He put our asses out. So, I had no choice but to take the girl home with me and wait for night to fall. By this time, the lil girl is whining, crying and screaming for her momma and shit, stressin' me the hell out. Just then, I get a phone call from this bad ass broad I've been wanting to fuck. She saying how she misses me, asking me where I been. Suddenly, she just breaks and tells me how bad she's been wanting the dick, but she had a man. After a little more conversation, she's begging me to come through to fuck her.

So, Lord forgive me," said Freddy, looking skyward. "I gagged the little girl, tied her up, and threw her in the closet."

"You what!" Coke yelled. "Damn, Freddy, how fucked up is that? For a piece of ass?"

"I know, Coke, man, I know. I fucked up. I'm sorry."

"Man... oh man, so finish. What else happened?"

"Okay, so after I leave the broad's house, it's dark. I'm ready to take the kid back to where I got her from, but when I get back home and opened the closet door, the girl was gone. I checked the house from top to bottom. The kid was nowhere to be found. Now, I'm scared than a muthafucka. I'm thinking all kinds of shit. Did she escape?

Nasty D!ck

Is she dead? Did the police find her? Shit, I even thought that maybe somebody kidnapped her from me. All I could think of was life in prison.

Then my cell phone rang. It was Ahbicdee talking some crazy shit, calling me a nasty-dick, child-molesting bitch. She just kept saying, 'You're going down, you're going down for this muthafucka!' Right then, Coke, it hit me. Ahbicdee must'a came home early and found the girl in the closet, but I'm playing stupid like I didn't know what's up. So, I ask her, 'What are you talking about?' but before she could answer, I heard something in the background sounding like CB radios and then her phone went dead."

"Did you try calling her back?" asked Coke, urgently.

"Yeah, I tried, but I kept getting her voicemail."

Coke began pacing the floor in frenzy, pointing at Freddy. "Awww, man. You fucked up this time! You fucked up real bad! You gon' have to fix this shit!"

"I know, Coke, man," he said, with his leg hanging over the arm of the chair.

Coke could see Freddy wasn't grasping the seriousness of the situation. He then one-hand-collared Freddy, pulling him up from the chair.

"No, muthafucka! Understand me! You gon' have to fix this shit! For all you know, your wife is at the police station giving them a statement against you about that girl. And your lame ass is just sitting here watching a flick of yourself fucking your wife's best friend."

He pushed Freddy back down into the chair.

"Get it together Freddy! Do you wanna end up dead? Do you want Ock and his people after yo' ass? 'Cause if this thang blows up, ain't no jail time for you. Your ass gon' be cut the fuck up and shipped off to ten different places around the world. This is no game."

Dex

Freddy had a better understanding now; an understanding of his life being at risk. He knew Coke was right. Ocknock and his associates were no joke. Many grave stories had been heard about their murderous actions, even stories of disfigurement.

There was one story rumored about a former abductor who was scheduled to testify against leaders of the international adoption ring, but before that could happen, his tongue was cut out and his hands were cut off. Therefore, he couldn't speak nor write any incriminating statements against no one.

Freddy shook with a quiver. "So, how can I fix this?" he asked, in desperation.

Coke gave him a dead serious look. "You really want to know? You can fix this by killing your wife."

"Killing my wife? Ahbicdee?"

"That's right. The bitch knows too much. Everything is now on the line; the agency, the hustle, and most of all, our freedom. She gotta go."

Freddy was distraught over what he was hearing. He couldn't believe the words coming out of Coke's mouth. "Wh, wh, what other choices do we have Coke?"

"None. That is the choice, or maybe we can roll on down to Ock's place and explain to him what happened."

Freddy took a moment to think it over. He then looked to Coke with questionable eyes.

"So, how do you suggest we kill her?"

Coke took a seat across from Freddy as he began to explain the murder plan.

Nasty D!ck

The Blue Room

The next day, Dex awoke. He walked down into the basement where he'd found Goose hanging a month ago. He was still in disbelief; still in question about if his favorite uncle was really dead. The obituary lying on the sofa confirmed it. *Damn,* sighed Dex, looking it over. *Ol' Goose. That was my man. Always kept his fronts up; never let you know when he was down.*

Dex grabbed a chair and stood in it, rubbing his hand across the beam, replaying the actions of how his uncle hung himself. As Dex stood in the chair, he noticed a shoebox stuffed high in the basement's corner. *What's that?* He took the chair over to where he'd seen the box. He stood in the chair again and pulled the box from its hiding place, setting it on the laundry table. When Dex opened the shoebox, he almost passed out. There were ten rolls of new bank bills with $10,000 markings on them.

He pulled a crisp one hundred-dollar from one of the packs, holding it up to the light, checking its authenticity.

"This shit is real!"

He kissed the bill and wondered where the money had come from. He then smiled.

Dex

"Uncle Goose must'a left the money for me and momma."

Suddenly, Dex heard footsteps coming down the basement stairs. He quickly stashed the shoebox. When he turned around, he jumped, startled by Coke's presence.

"How did you get in here?" Dex asked, aggressively.

"Why do you have that stupid-ass look on your face?" Coke fired back. He then gave Dex a suspicious look. "You look like you're up to something," with a raised eyebrow.

"I ain't up to nothing," denied Dex, standing in between the washer and dryer, sliding the box backward with his foot.

Coke dismissed it telling Dex they needed to talk. The two sat down on the couch. Coke got straight to the point.

"I need you to kill somebody for me. The job pays $30,000."

"Kill somebody!" screeched Dex's voice. "I ain't 'bout to kill nobody. What did they do to you?"

Coke sighed. He then took a different approach. "Dex, what are you gonna do with your life? You…"

Dex interrupted. "I know, I know. We done had this discussion many times. I'm thirty-five, I've got seven kids, I'm broke, I live with my momma, and I only have pussy on the brain. I'm tired of hearing that shit Coke. I've got plans. You don't have to worry about me no more. Just take care of yourself!"

Coke could see that Dex had suddenly grown cocky. "Oh, so you've got plans, now, huh?"

"Yup," said Dex, shaking his head confidently.

"And I don't need to worry about you no more, right?"

"Nope. Not at all," he responded, again shaking his head.

"Yeah, well I hope your plans don't include that $100,000 you found in that shoebox in the corner. That's my money," Coke grimmed.

Dex's mouth dropped. "That's right. And how could you have thought that Goose left y'all anything? He was a bum and you know it. That dude couldn't piss straight in the toilet."

Dex tried to disguise his disappointment over the money. Coke then eased to the edge of his seat.

"Listen Dex, I'm offering you the opportunity to make some good money here. What I'm asking of you ain't that hard. You lay this broad down for me and you get paid. Real simple."

"A broad? It's a female?" asked Dex, feeling at ease.

"Oh, did I fail to mention it was a *woman* that needed to be done? And guess whose wife she is? Freddy's."

Dex's face wrinkled up. "Freddy! You fuckin' with him?"

"Yeah, I'm fucking with him. He's the reason why that shoebox is stacked like it is, and it's gon' be many more to follow. Freddy and I have a decent business relationship but don't get it twisted, Dex. I know Freddy's a snake. I haven't forgot that he played you over Flower some years back. I figured this was just a way you could get a little payback and make some money."

Dex understood everything Coke was saying and he definitely wanted some payback against Freddy.

"Okay, Coke, I'll do it. I'll take this broad out for you, but only under one condition."

"And what is that?"

Dex

"After I do this, I want you to take Freddy out for me. And whatever business venture you two are involved in, I want his spot."

Coke smiled. "Shit, you ain't said nothing. That was the plan anyway."

Coke then counted out $5,000, laying it on top of the washing machine. "Take this money Dex. Have a little fun. Go and buy your kids something."

Dex was grateful. He hadn't had this type of money since his last income tax refund. Coke finished with a last word.

"I told you, Dex. I got you. I'm all you need. You and I are one. Without you, there is no me."

****

At this time, Freddy and Ahbicdee were in a heated discussion over why the girl was tied up in their closet. Freddy explained as much as he could, careful not to mention the adoption agency. He danced around several questions and got caught up in a few lies.

After being verbally scolded for his actions, he tried to make Ahbicdee feel as if she was responsible for what happened. Freddy was good at using reverse psychology on his wife but this time, she wasn't buying it.

"Uh, uh, Freddy, you dirty bastard," she said, pointing, with a dish-rag in her hand. "I'll be damned if you make me feel some guilt over your devilish deeds. You chose to do what you do on your own. I didn't have nothing to do with that. You're taking this heat by yourself. Snatching kids and carrying on, you disgust me." She then turned up her nose, giving him the evil eye.

Like anyone who was wrong, Freddy was offended.

Nasty D!ck

"Disgust you! Bitch! How in the fuck you think you've been eating? How in the hell you think this house and that luxury car you drive is being paid for, huh? I don't see you making nothing around here except some burnt up ass chicken. Don't be so quick to dismiss yourself from this. You're guilty too, just as guilty as I am. And don't get me started on what you came from," ready to read Ahbicdee her life story. But, with a second thought, Freddy rephrased his words, not wanting to make the situation worse.

"And *heat* you say? You brought the heat your damn self! When you found that girl in the closet tied up, why didn't you call me? You could have easily called me and asked, Freddy, do you have a little girl tied up in our closet? I would have told you, yes. But noooo…, you chose to be an honorary citizen and take her down to the police station yourself."

Ahbicdee defended herself. "I told you Freddy, I didn't take that girl to the police station. I took her to Child Protective Services. I told them I found the girl wandering the streets. And it must've been one of their CB radios you heard in the background just before my phone went dead, but believe me Freddy, I would never put your freedom at risk."

Freddy flopped down in his recliner, cocking his leg over the arm of the chair. He knew his wife might have been telling the truth. Nonetheless, he wanted to make her feel guilty, just because he knew he could. He threw his hand up.

"Whatever, Ahbicdee. You ain't gotta butter me up. I'll know the truth after I go to bed tonight and the police come busting in here and take my black ass off to jail. I'm gon' do twenty years hard time because of you!"

Dishes crumbled and glass broke. Ahbicdee stomped out of the kitchen in frustration, throwing the wet dish-rag, striking Freddy in the back of his head. Standing at the

Dex

closet, she put on her coat, hat, and sunglasses, and grabbed her purse.

Freddy rose up in the recliner. "Hey, hey! Where are you going? I ain't through talking to you. Get back in here!" Ahbicdee threw up her middle finger, slamming the front door shut behind her.

Freddy then laid back in his chair, snickering. *Yup, she feels guilty,* he thought, with no worries. He knew exactly where Ahbicdee was going. She was running straight to her best friend, Ché's house to confide in her; to tell her the truth about everything that transpired.

He also knew that shortly thereafter, he would receive a call from Ché, who would inform him of everything that was discussed there.

Freddy chuckled. *I got this on lock.* He then looked at Ahbicdee's picture hanging on the wall, speaking to it.

"It ain't that you know too much, baby. It's just that, I'm tired of yo' ass."

****

The day fell into the night. The $5,000 Dex received from Coke was burning a hole in his pocket. He spent two hundred dollars apiece on his children, but not before purchasing himself a brand new wardrobe. He bought designer jeans, polo shirts, gym shoes, slacks, a few button up shirts, and a pair of loafers. He also treated his mother to a bottle of perfume.

Dex didn't have a special lady in his life but he planned on hitting every female's house that he was sexing just to show her how clean he could get. After trying on his third outfit, Dex stepped to the mirror for a look. He turned side to side, checking his profile. The Phat Farm outfit he was sporting draped as if it was tailored for his body. He had forgotten how new clothes could make a man feel. He then rubbed on some lotion, sprayed on a little cologne and counted his money.

"Damn, I only got $800 left?" he counted, looking at the clothes spread out on his bed. "Fuck it," hunching his shoulders. "I've got $25,000 more coming anyway."

Downstairs, Barbara thanked Dex as he handed her the bottle of perfume.

"It smells so nice," inhaling the sweet fragrance. "But it ain't income tax time. Looks like somebody done ran into a few dollars."

"Things are looking up, Ma."

Barbara squint her eye. "Are they now?"

Aww, shit. She got that look on her face.

"So, Dex, are you still working?"

Just out the blue. Am I working?

Dex smirked, shaking his head, remaining silent, figuring she already knew the answer. Barbara then pulled out his termination letter from work.

"This is dated back six months ago and according to this Dex, you don't have a job. And if you don't have a job, that means you're not in therapy."

Barbara then went off, screaming to the top of her lungs. As she continued lecturing Dex, he tuned her out.

How in the hell did she find that letter? I hid it well, deep in the attic behind the wall insulation. Shit, in fact, right where I keep all my nude photos, but she ain't said nothing about the pictures yet. Dex stood confused.

Just then, Barbara stomped her foot.

"Do you understand me?" she asked for the third time.

Dex

Dex came to. "Understand what?" he whined, never hearing the question.

"I said, whether you know it or not, you're a sick man, son. And I'm not prepared to deal with your illness any longer. I don't have the emotional or physical strength to cope with it. It's too hard on me, and besides, I'm still dealing with the loss of my brother. Dex, if you don't get back on your medication and seek the therapy you need, then I'm sorry son, you're gonna have to find somewhere else to live." She then walked away.

Dex snatched his mother's car keys off the table.

"I ain't got no illness and I don't need no therapy. I just wanna make some money and fuck all day. What's wrong with that?" he mumbled, walking out of the house.

Dex was driving to visit his lady friend when he passed The Purple Slip Gentlemen's Club.

"I haven't been there in years," looking in his rear view mirror. He made a u-turn and pulled into the parking lot. The neon lights made the joint look inviting. He entered the club.

"Five dollar entry, baby," said the woman behind the 3-inch glass. Dex couldn't see the woman's face, but he saw her large breasts, and that was enough. He paid the five-dollar entry fee and tipped the woman an extra five bucks. "Thanks. Have fun," she said.

"Oh, trust me, I will."

Dex opened the entry door to the main floor. He smiled in disbelief. Ass-naked women were everywhere. Short women, tall women, thick women, slim women. Big assess, small asses, some with no asses. There was no limit. To Dex, it was just a big ol' pot of pussy.

"Woooo...wee! I don't remember all this ass the last time I was here!"

As Dex stood getting into the groove and sipping on his drink, one of the ladies passing by rubbed his dick through his pants. Another one passing behind him caressed his ass.

"Damn, is it me or is this just what they do here?" Flattered by the attention, he again checked his profile in the mirror. Right then, Dex and the finest woman he'd seen tonight made eye contact. The woman was five-foot-eight, with short hair. She had a model's jaw line, sensuous lips, and a walk that would make an old man piss on himself.

"Hi sugar," she greeted, coming face-to-face with Dex. "Buy me a drink?"

Dex took a step back, admiring her naked body. He could picture himself latching onto her titties and start sucking.

"Girl, with that body you got, I'd buy you the whole bar." She giggled, extending her hand.

"My name is Sin. I was hoping that you and I could grab a room and maybe, commit one." The direct invite for sex had Dex's dick rock hard. He was just about to inquire the price when..., "I'm just kidding," she grinned. "I'm a tease at times."

"Really, you shouldn't do that," countered Dex with a playful, but serious look.

After introducing himself and buying her that drink, Dex invited her over to the couch.

"Right here, baby. Sit next to me," he rubbed the spot.

Before Sin sat down, she placed a towel on the couch to sit on. Dex couldn't help but to stare at her pussy lips

Dex

tucked between her thighs as she sat down. He closed his eyes in ecstasy.

The two conversed for an hour. She was really enjoying Dex's conversation. She felt he was pretty smooth, despite his eyes periodically dropping down into her lap, but she liked it. The attention made her pussy wet, and on top of that, Dex had already tipped her $200, and she hadn't done a thing but talk. Sin knew conversation only went so far. She then uncrossed her legs and, slyly, stroked her clit. Her middle finger was soaking wet. She started rubbing her finger around her bottom lip, slowly licking it. She then widened her tongue and began working her finger in and out of her mouth like she was sucking a dick.

"Do you like that, Dex?" giving him the, *I will suck yo' dick* eyes. Dex was ready to explode.

"Hell, yeah, I like that. What's up with it?" he asked, wanting to pull out his dick.

Sin waved her finger, *No*. She, again, rubbed her clit, this time waving her finger around Dex's nose.

"No scent," she bragged.

Dex then grabbed her finger, sucking it.

"And it tastes great," he added.

Sin didn't expect that. Her clit heightened. A mini-orgasm tingled through her body. She felt the wetness from her pussy seep between the crack of her ass. It made her want to invite Dex inside her love.

Right then, Dex again grabbed her hand, spreading her two fingers. He stuck his tongue between her fingers, pretending it was her pussy. He licked, sucked and slurped as if he really was between her thighs.

Sin's tongue did slow laps across her teeth. She quietly groaned, moving her fingers in circles over her breasts. She never knew finger sucking could be so exhilarating, wishing his juicy lips were below her waistline. Just then, Sin lost her good sense. She locked into a deep kiss with Dex, sucking his tongue, kissing him like she wanted to fuck the shit out of him, pinching and stroking the head of his dick from the outside of his pants, while at the same time, massaging his balls.

Dex again peered downward into her lap at what appeared to be coconut juice dripping from her clit. He slowly placed his hand on her inner thigh, cupping her pussy, straddling his finger along her warm slit. Within seconds, Sin started to cum. She hummed harmoniously in Dex's mouth, grinding her hips.

Dex firmly pinned her clitoris between his finger and thumb, increasing her junky-like convulsions. When Sin came down off her 30-second orgasmic high, she stood up and walked away. Dex sat puzzled.

"What the hell! Where is she going? I gotta get mine, too," hand dripping wet.

The towel and part of the couch was drenched as well. Sin came walking back with fresh towels.

"Are you okay?" asked Dex, while wiping his hand, pretending like he didn't know she had came.

Sin placed her hand on her chest.

"Dex, you bring new life to a girl," grabbing his hand. "C'mon, let's go to the Blue Room."

The Blue Room? thought Dex. *Oh yeah... it's time to fuck!*

They approached a door just past the restrooms. Sin knocked on the door. A pair of eyes appeared in a rectangular opening on the door. The eyes looked to Sin, then to Dex.

"He's with me," she nodded, referring to Dex.

Dex

The door opened. Sin walked past the guard. Dex was following closely when the guard stopped him, by the chest.

"It's a $25 entry fee."

Dex paid the money, ready to walk in. The guard stopped him again. "That's $25 each, for the both of you."

Twenty-five dollars each? Shiiiid... I just bought fifty dollars worth of drinks and tipped Sin's ass two hundred dollars and my dick ain't been nowhere near the pussy, Dex wanted to say.

Sin saw Dex's hesitation and gave him a look as if he were a cheapskate. "Oh, I didn't know another $25 was gon' hurt yo' pockets. I'm sorry. I can pay my own way," she said, reaching inside her moneybag.

Dex sighed, feeling he'd just been put on front-street. Sin's offer to pay her own way made him feel bold.

"Naw, naw, I got it. It's no problem at all," claimed Dex as he paid the guard, thinking, *All this money I'm spending, this pussy better be some fire!*

When Dex stepped further inside the Blue Room, he was disappointed. The room wasn't blue at all. It was white. There were no beds or mattresses, not even a pallet on the floor, and plus, there were about 20 other people in the room sitting in folding chairs in front of a stage.

"What the hell is this?" asked Dex, wanting his money back. "I thought the Blue Room was the fucking room. I don't want to see no show."

Sin read the irritation on Dex face. "Trust me love, this will be one of the greatest experiences of your life," leading him to a pair of front row seats.

Whatever, thought Dex, looking around the room, seeing dancers seated with others suckers just like him.

Nasty D!ck

The room suddenly went dark and the stage lit up. Forest green lighting appeared in the background behind a woman on stage sitting in a chair with her head tilted backwards.

"The Forbidden Fruit!" echoed a man's voice from the loudspeakers throughout the room.

An apple began lowering from a chain down towards the woman on stage. Her mouth was wide open, ready to take a bite.

"No…! No…! Don't do it! Don't eat the forbidden fruit!" shouted the onlookers in the crowd.

Sin was also yelling to *Blossom,* the woman on the stage not to eat the fruit.

This is some corny bullshit, thought Dex, with his arms folded.

Finally, the apple reached Blossom's mouth. She snatched the apple from the chain and bit into it. Suddenly, the stage went dark.

"What the fuck?" whispered Dex to Sin. "Is that it? For fifty bucks?"

"Shhhhh! It's not over yet," squeezing his thigh.

Within thirty seconds, the stage lit up again, this time with royal blue lighting.

"That's a nice color," said Dex.

What was even more mesmerizing was Blossom, who was lying naked in bed on the stage. Her legs were spread wide open. As she lay, a man came walking onto the stage. His large dick was swinging back and forth like an elephant's trunk.

"Whew…!" chimed the ladies in the audience, now on their feet.

"That's what I'm talking about, girl!" yelled one woman. "Twelve inches of dick!"

Dex

"Bust 'em down, Blossom!" cheered others.

Dex wasn't gay or had any tendencies of being gay but in his mind along with a few other brothers in the audience, the man on stage had a big dick.

The man approached Blossom. She lifted from the bed.

"Have a bite of my apple?" she offered to him.

No!" he turned away. "It is the forbidden fruit. It causes mischief and sexual desires."

"Oh, but you are wrong, misguided one. Forbidden fruit, it is not," she lied. "Bite and see."

She's lyin', thought Dex, eyes glued on the stage.

After a brief pause, the man bit into the apple. The apple fell from his hand. He then grabbed Blossom, locking into a kiss. Afterwards, he picked her up, straddled her feet around his waist, and slipped his large dick inside her dripping wet pussy.

As if he were a carousel, he slowly stroked her body up and down on his slippery pole, suspending her in the air, palming her ass in his hands like a bowl of cherries.

Dex was so into what was going on, he found himself jerking his hips as if it was he on the stage fucking. From the excitement, Sin again, moistened her towels.

Just then, another man appeared on stage with a larger dick than the first man.

"It's horse dick!" someone yelled. The ladies in the crowd went wild.

"Hell naw!! That can't be real!"

"He gon' kill her with that dick he got!"

"Oh, my God!"

The women in the audience all commented about how they would never fuck a dick that big. They joked, saying that after a round with Horse, you would need a pussy transplant.

Horse approached. "What is the act you two perform?"

"It is called fuckin'," emphasized the first man. "Would you like to join in?"

"No, it sounds painful, but I would like to have a bite of your fruit," pointing to the apple.

"Go ahead."

After Horse bit into the apple, Blossom found herself with two large dicks in each of her hands.

Oh shit, this muthafucka' got a big ass dick, thought Blossom. *This is the type of dick you throw up off of trying to deep throat it. The type of dick that fucks your insides all up, make a bitch have to make a doctor's appointment afterwards. I can handle Quinn, but this Horse muthafucka' ain't gettin' up in me, not with all that. I'ma have to bust him down sucking his dick. Lucky for me, my throat game is platinum, worth a million.*

Blossom started off sucking Quinn's dick like a car wash power vac, hitting it from all angles. She sucked the left side of his dick, the right side, the head, and again from the left. She then gripped his ass, stabbing herself in the tonsils, trying to make him bust quick, not knowing he had staying power.

Before long, Horse laid his dick upon her lips, fighting for some of the attention. He stretched her mouth wide open with his dick-and-a-half, placing his hand on top of her head. Blossom was somewhat intimidated by his massive cock, but was up to the challenge. She slowly, worked the head, holding on with both hands. Her soft lips retracted back and forth, searching for his spot, licking the secretions of semen from his tip.

Dex

After a minute or two of working with it, Blossom got back into her comfort zone. She began to view Horse's dick like any other. She began having fun with it, taking him in deep, but still only getting him halfway in, as Horse pressed further toward the back of her throat. Nearly choking, Blossom pulled his dick from her mouth.

"Okay now, this ain't no pussy you in," she reminded him, sliding him back in and out the sides of her jaw. Her mouth was sopping wet, making those slurpy, sucking, smacking sounds a hot, wet tongue makes.

Horse began showing signs of buckling down. His facial expressions and heavy breathing were snatching away his mask. Blossom knew it was only a matter of seconds. She sucked faster. Horse was moaning like a bitch, at the point when he releasing his nut. Blossom was slapping his dick against her tongue, ready to receive her gift.

Dex wanted to see Horse cum in her mouth. Sin wanted to see Horse cum on her face. The ladies in the audience just wanted to see Horse cum. But like a jealous baby fighting for a tit, Quinn broke the connection, easing his way back into Blossom's mouth. Before she knew it, there was a battle for her tonsils.

Both Quinn and Horse's hands were on top of her head, giving it to her; bumping dicks, one trying to out stroke the other. Abdominal muscles and nuts were slapping her face as if she'd committed a crime. As far as Blossom was concerned, a crime was being committed—against her.

Two dicks? In my mouth? At the same time? Hell no! My ex-husband, with his smooth talkin' ass, couldn't have even convinced me to do no shit like this!

Blossom spit both dicks from her mouth and stood up from the bed. "Damn Quinn! Horse! Just dog me out! Shit! I'm trying to put on a live porno show for the folks here

Nasty D!ck

watching, but god...damn! I'm not about to let y'all kill me tryin' to doin' it. A bitch choking; I can't breathe; my jaws are all stretched out and shit. I mean, where does my fun come in at, my satisfaction? My titties are hard. My pussy is wet, and all you two can do about it is fuck me in my mouth. I'm through, show's over," she looked to the audience.

"Awww," moaned the freaks from the audience, rising from their seats.

Everyone was disappointed, especially Dex. Sin was right. This was one of the greatest experiences of his life. He'd experienced many threesomes in his time, but had never sat back and watched one. He was the last to leave his chair.

Blossom was bending over the bed looking for her earrings when she felt arms wrap around her waist. From the back, her vaginal slit was filled with warm, hard, nature. She moaned from the fit. The freaks rushed back to their chairs.

As horse lay on his back being rode like the horse that he was, Quinn stood over Blossom's back. He rolled his black snake around the back of her neck, laying it over her shoulder. He then massaged her back with it as he dropped down to his knees. He whispered some erotic and exotic shit while nibbling on her ear. Whatever it was, it made her pussy wetter.

Horse pulled Blossom down towards him by her shoulders. Her beautiful brown asshole was up in the air for the taking. Quinn lubricated his shaft, while watching Blossom do squats over Horse's dick. The scene was beautiful. Quinn wanted to prep that ass with his tongue but it was too close to she and Horse's business at hand.

Quinn crawled up and gently eased in the head. Blossom moaned and groaned erotically. She couldn't believe two large dicks were in her soul. The pain was excruciating, but it hurt so good. She was turned—the fuck—on.

Whew! She's a better bitch than I am, thought Sin.

Quinn took mini-strokes, squeezing himself the rest of the way in, as Horse beat and thrust himself up in Blossom's 125-pound frame. Sweat ran down her back. Cum oozed from her clit. Saliva dripped from her lips. Quinn was all in her shit. Blossom felt she could get no higher. The word, *"Cum"* escaped through her teeth.

To accommodate her request, Quinn latches his hands over her shoulders just alongside Horse's grip. He pushed faster and harder, reaching peak depth inside her ass. Blossom reached under, feeling the soaked wetness from her pussy and the two dicks and balls crashing against both of her holes. She slid her nasty ass fingers into Horse's mouth, letting him taste her juice. Horse squeezed the muscles in his ass while sucking her fingers, again feeling his nut coming on. Blossom pulled out his dick, kissing it, licking it, and ejaculating him at the same time.

Quinn, too, was ready to release an ounce inside of her ass. Then, one after the other, the babies flew, the white birds chirped and the screams of passion were heard. Nuts were bust, sexual appetites were filled, and the trio, all then lay in the bed as the stage again went dark.

Nasty D!ck

Getting Caught

"Girl... from everything you've just told me, husband or not, sounds like the police needs to be called," encouraged Ché for the third time.

"No Ché, that's the last thing I'm going to do," claimed Ahbicdee. "I told you, Freddy's not a bad man. He's just..."

He's just what Ahbicdee? Say it! He's just a muthafuckin' dog and you know it. The man can't keep his dick in his pants. I don't know how you put up with his ass. I can't count how many times you've came over here crying 'cause of some shit he's done to you. What about that time he was messing around with your next door neighbor?"

Ahbicdee closed her eyes, cupping her face.

"Lord, don't remind me," shaking her head.

"Don't remind you? How could you forget it?" hunched Ché. "That woman's husband was gonna shoot you and Freddy's ass."

"I had to protect my husband."

"Protect your husband from what, fuckin' your neighbor? How about your husband protecting his wife, and

Dex

taking that infidelity shit elsewhere if that's what he chooses to do. Or, what about the time..."

Ahbicdee heard it coming, cutting Ché short.

"Don't you even say it Ché. I already know."

"Well if you know, then it shouldn't matter. The time Freddy fucked back around with his ex-wife Flower?"

Ahbicdee deeply sighed. Memory lane was taking a toll on her nerves.

"Now you know we can't let that one die!" roared Ché. "Freddy knew that bitch was crazy times three from when they were married. That's why he divorced her ass. And to go back messing around with her after what, after 15 years of divorce? What kind of shit is that? And to make matters worse, he gets tangled up with another bitch, who claims to be Flower's woman, who he met in a three-some, who then claimed Freddy got her pregnant. You remember that, right?"

Ahbicdee nodded a distant, *Yes.*

Ché continued. "And Flower and her girl, I can't think of that bitch name, extorted Freddy out about seven or eight thousand dollars, all 'cause he was trying to keep the girl's pregnancy a secret from you. But you end up finding out anyway, because Freddy was mad and couldn't keep his mouth closed about how the girl really wasn't pregnant and how they played his stupid ass out of his money."

Silence whisked the room. Only the furnace could be heard running.

Ahbicdee was feeling worse than when she first came to Ché's house. She wanted to break down and cry. She wanted Ché's shoulder to lean on, but it was time out for that. Ché was right. Freddy had done some horrid things to her over the years. Things she knew she didn't deserve. Things Ché knew nothing of. True, Freddy did have relations

81

Nasty D!ck

with his neighbor's wife, but he had also had relations with their eighteen-year-old daughter that wasn't mentioned. The girl confessed in an apology letter to Ahbicdee after they moved away. There was another incident where Freddy brought another woman into their home. Freddy had offered his lady friend a drink of wine as the two conversed. Freddy not knowing Ahbicdee had returned home from a two-day stay away after she and Freddy had an argument, was half way up the stairs when the rose scent of bubble bath lingered across his nose. Ahbicdee in the bathtub paused, unsure if she heard voices. She then called Freddy's name. There was no answer, but Ahbicdee was no fool. She sprung from her bath, throwing on her robe, running downstairs. There was no sign of Freddy, no glasses of wine, or any woman. Only the aroma of perfume was left in the air. When confronted with the issue, Freddy swore on his grave he was never there.

Ché saw Ahbicdee's pain in the different facial expressions she was making. She could tell Ahbicdee's mind was racing at a 100 miles per hour. Ché's mind began to drift inside of her own thoughts.

That's my girl Ahbicdee over there, my friend since ten-years old. She's been leaning on my shoulder for a long time now; almost three decades, ever since her daddy just one day up and left. I've always been there for her. I've always been her rock; her shoulder to lean on. I'm a strong woman most of the time, I know this, but at other times, I falls weak myself. Where's my shoulder to lean on, my shoulder to cry a tear on? Who's my rock? I so many times ask myself. That's why I can't stand Ahbicdee's ass sometimes. This bitch got a man but always whining and crying; always running to me; Freddy did this, Freddy did that. Whew... I get sick of hearing that shit. I sometimes be wanting to tell her to shut the fuck up, woman up and handle that shit. You don't need him if you can't handle him. I came this close one day to telling Ahbicdee how good Freddy eats my pussy; how he fucks me until I can't see straight, and then how he eats my pussy again. That man does wonders with his tongue. And his dick, oh... it's just so pretty. I love how he drives it in and out my mouth. And when he puts it in me, my body secretes with cum until I reach the point of dehydration. 'Juicy Fruit,' is what Freddy hisses, as he slips in and out the depth of my slippery lining. Far as I'm concerned, he's my man to share. I mean... I would like to have a man of my own; a man to wake up to in the morning; smell his morning breath; sniff under his armpit; maybe even suck his dick before he awakes. A man who I could cook for; do his laundry; someone who I could take care of that is my own. And as fine as I am, I should have that. But instead, my stupid ass is caught up with my best friend's man. I can recall the day it happened...

Ding Dong! The doorbell rang. Ahbicdee in the bathtub sat straight up. "Shit, I'm late. Freddy! That's Ché!" reaching for her towel. "Open the door! Tell her I'll be ready in a minute!"

Freddy watching TV got up from his chair.

"Ass ain't nev'a on time for nothing," he mumbled opening the door. Ché walked in looking like the flavor of the month. She had on her leopard print skirt, a black low cut shirt exposing the top of her breast, her black boots which stopped just below the knee, accessorized with her Cartier earrings and bracelet to match. The bitch was fly. Freddy agreed as well as he did a triple take looking Ché up and down.

"God... damn Ché, you're a fine muthafucka'," stroking his goatee.

Nasty D!ck

"Thank you," Ché smiled, always appreciating Freddy's compliments.

"Mmm mmph, and them boots look sexy ass hell on you too. Model them for me, walk across the room.

Ché blushed as she walked back and forth across the living room floor. Freddy was checking out her strong calf muscle imprint through her boots.

Ahbicdee came out of the bathroom wrapped in a towel. "I'll be dressed in a minute Ché," she hollered down, rushing to her bedroom.

"Take your time, it's no rush. I'll be in the refrigerator," responded Ché in a model's stance. She then strolled back past Freddy who inhaled the scent of her perfume. "Ssmm... Aahh..."

Damn Ché smells good. I've been checking her out for the past five years. This bitch is fine. She's the one who I should've gotten with; good job, makes her own money, never complains and she looks like she got some good pussy. And them lips, eeww... them lips just make me wanna, damn..." squeezing the head of this dick, feeling himself getting hard. *I know Ché wants me like I want her. I can tell by how she looks at me; how she holds conversations with me even after I tell her Ahbicdee isn't home. I'ma hit that.*"

Right then, Ché's earring fell from her ear in front of Freddy. They both looked to the earring, afterwards at one another. The unspoken chemistry was there. The two in a sly manner then looked to the upstairs. Freddy unzipped his pants. Ché lifted her skirt, bending over, slowly pulling her panties to the side. Freddy's pants fell around his ankles. He then gripped Ché's hip, sliding his hot stick inside her wet love. He smashed, bashed and crashed that ass with everything he had, literally trying to push his nuts inside of her. Even though it was a quickie, Freddy was putting his

Dex

best fuck forward. He wanted to leave an impressionable stain on Ché's brain. It would be shameful and embarrassing for her to have cheated with her best friend's man and the sex is weak, plus Freddy wanted to fuck her again.

Ché's mouth was hung open. She could feel the power strokes from that hard dick crushing her walls. Her body jerked forward from every thrust. Pussy juice was leaking down the insides of her legs. The dick was everything Ahbicdee had claimed it to be, and some. Ché was impressed, as much as she was excited, ready to bust, when...

"Ok girl, I'm finally ready!" marched Ahbicdee through the upstairs hallway.

Freddy with his dick still inside of Ché who was bent over the couch, crept into the kitchen, steering her hands onto the edge of the sink. There, he again started fucking her. Ahbicdee was now walking down the stairs. Ché was scared to death.

"She's coming... Ahbicdee's coming!" she uttered in a whisper trying to pull from Freddy's grip, but his hold was tight, feeling a massive nut coming on. He kept on stroking with no regard. It was as if he wanted to get caught.

Ahbicdee standing in the living room looked around the room, puzzled. "Ché! Freddy?" she called listening for any sounds. "Freddy!" There was no response.

Freddy with his hand over Ché's mouth was in a slow grind releasing himself.

After not seeing or hearing anyone, Ahbicdee walked around into the kitchen. She folded her arms.

"I see you found what you were looking for Ché!"

Ché lifted up, closing the refrigerator door. "Ahbicdee, you know I love me some yogurt," grabbing a spoon.

Nasty D!ck

Freddy stomped the last two basement steps counting money as if just came from his stash spot.

"Here," handing Ahbicdee $500.

"$500?" she questioned. "I only needed $50. We're just going out for a couple of drinks."

Freddy weak in the knees flopped back in his chair in front of the TV. "Don't worry about it. You and Ché have a good time on me."

Ahbicdee looked to Ché shrugging her shoulders. "Ok, thanks."

After that, Ahbicdee and I left out the door. As usual, she never suspected a thing. I sometimes get chills just thinking how close Freddy and I came to getting caught. That man lives on the edge. But then, it saddens me to know when I look at him, he is the father of my unborn child.

Suddenly, Ahbicdee stood up in a roar. "That muthafuckin' Freddy don't care about me! I seriously doubt if he really ever loved me! You're right Ché, the police needs to be involved. Freddy's gonna get his this time. Ol' baby snatching son-of-a-bitch! You got my back, right?" she eyed Ché.

"No doubt," assured Ché.

"Ok, I first have to put a few things in place. I'll get back with you when it's time."

Ahbicdee then headed out the front door. Ché didn't hesitate to call Freddy.

Dex

Love Don't Live Here Anymore

Two weeks had passed and Dex was spending money at an alarming rate. He'd ran through another $15,000 since taking on the company of his lost childhood lover Flower, and her girlfriend Sin. Together these two women took Dex to sexual heights he couldn't begin to imagine; opening doors to fantasy worlds he never knew existed, witnessing in this short time span, twosomes, threesomes, quartets and even a 30-man orgy, participating in them all. They were turning Dex out, and spending his cash. He even one day found himself naked outfitted in a fruit salad fashion, layered in chocolate syrup and covered with every fruit imaginable. Ten women including Flower and Sin feasted on this human dessert delicacy. From the pineapple rings that they nibbled from around his penis, to the multiple nuts he bust in their mouths, everything was devoured, Dex was licked clean. Flower then ordered all the women down onto the floor into the doggy style position. She commanded Dex to have sex with every one of them not for more than one minute. The offer was overwhelming, a proposal no man would turn down, but Dex claimed of weariness from his numerous orgasms he'd had in the last couple of weeks. Flower wouldn't hear of it. She gave him two blue pills, *Viagra* to rejuvenate him, more than enough to jump-start any mans engine. After twenty minutes of recovery, Dex went at it trying to satisfy them all. He sexed six of the women until he again succumb to the excitement of this attempt.

Before long, another 30 minutes had passed, Dex was miserably rock hard. He was hard to the point where he ached. Still, it didn't detour the arousing feeling he had watching the one on one between Flower and Sin.

"Eeewww... Eew... Right there, right there baby, don't stop," moaned Sin spreading her ass checks further apart. From the back, Flower's face was planted in Sin's ass.

Sop! Sop! Smack! Sop! sounded Sin's pussy with every lick and suck Flower made.

"Uh...! Uh...! Uh...!"

The sheets cringed in Sin's hands. She arched her back like a camel trying to escape that vicious tongue, but Flower strong-armed her hips back into place.

Damn, Flowers eatin' the shit out of Sin's pussy, thought Dex. *I need to be taking some notes.*

He sat onto the edge of the bed closely watching. Flower's lips were in a fury, pulling at Sin's clit like a fish on a hook, showing no signs of letting loose. Afterwards, she slipped her tongue into Sin's ass. Sin began taking erratic breaths, biting and ripping into the bed spread, screaming Flower's name.

"Eewww baby! Eeww baby!" feeling convulsions throughout her body.

Damn... These are some real freaks.

Dex turned on, inched closer. He wanted in on this sexual escapade. He gently caressed Sin's back, down to the crack of her ass and back up around her neck. Sin was loving Dex's warm touch, along with Flower's hot, steamy tongue.

Dex

Sin then whispered, "I want you to fuck me Dex. I want your long black dick inside of me," licking up and down his thighs.

Flower repositioned herself on the bed, just under Sin's perky breast. She loved biting and sucking on those black nipples. Sin bent over, felt Dex slapping his hard meat against her butt cheeks.

"C'mon Dex, quit teasing. Put it in," begged Sin.

Dex wanted to fuck her bad, but he had another idea, some super freaky shit. He instead slipped himself inside of Flower. He then had Sin stand onto her legs and squat in an A-style position, aligning her pussy with his face. The eight other women stood aside watching this sexually intense, acrobatic show. Dex was fucking Flower and licking Sin where Flower left off.

Flower was French kissing Sin, pinching and pulling on her breast. Sin was loving it all, hoping her legs and arms didn't give out.

"C'mon Dex, fuck me! Fuck me! Damn, is it even in me?" Flower joked, sucking on Sin's titties.

Dex smirked as he teased Sin's clit. *Ol' freak bitch Flower got jokes I see. I can't help it 'cause she's use to elephant dicks like horse's being all up in her. I ain't about to fuck myself into a coma trying to dig down in her bottomless hole. This broad is crazy. Besides, being around Flower for these past two weeks have been fun but unbearable. The bitch thinks she's some type of Madame or female pimp or something. True, she knows a lot of fine ass women that will do some out cold freaky shit. But it's my dollar that's making all this possible. $2000 for eight of these freaky live hoes for two hours was worth it. I paid Flower the money, who claimed the price was $3000 but one of the girls had slipped up and told me the actual price. It's*

Nasty D!ck

cool, I ain't mad, Flower hustled me, but after today, I'm through with her ass. I did what I wanted to do with her ten times over. She's a great fuck, but I'm not feeling her as a person. She's too bossy and very controlling, money hungry too. I don't know what Freddy saw in her ass to make him marry her. I guess two snakes can live in one den. But Sin, I like her. I wouldn't mind keeping her for myself. Her pussy is snug, tight and stays hell'a wet. I can feel her walls grip my dick when I drive it in and out that ass. I even came in her a few times. I couldn't help it, the pussy's good. Fuck it, I got seven kids already anyway, what's one more gon' hurt? Besides, Sin's cute with a beautiful personality and about ten years younger than Flower. I can deal with that. But Flower, a childhood lost love? Ha! Far as I'm concerned, that bitch can get lost forever, Dex continued stroking, as if he never had such thoughts.

Flower tongue licking with Sin, eyed Dex with her own personal thoughts. *Dex thinks he's slick with his ancient ass. He wants my girl, Sin. I see it all in his eyes. The way he kisses her, rubs her back, just his whole demeanor. He got this fuck thang confused. I bet'cha his dumb-ass is too naive to know I'm even paying attention. It don't surprise me, Dex was never really one to see shit even though it be right there in his face. Mmph, he thought I wasn't fucking back when I was with him. Shit, Freddy and I had been creeping around on Dex for nearly two years. Freddy would always tell me about some of the crazy shit Dex use to do. In fact, I remember Dex being a little off back then myself, now that I think about it. Talking to himself, answering back, getting violent and shit. He even called himself another name one day. Yeah... Dex was a nutcase. That's why I left him alone. And the fact that he messed around with his uncle's bitch on me, Catwalk. Since these past two weeks, I haven't seen any*

Dex

psychotic signs. He must be better now. But from what I'm seeing, Dex pockets are long. This boy is handling some dollars. He's spending money like it's nothing to him. He paid $3000 for eight bad bitches I know. And of course, I made my cut; I put this shit together. Sin's my bitch, but as long as Dex is spending money like he is, I'ma put my personal feelings aside. He can kiss her, caress her, fuck her, do all that shit. But after that money is made at the end of the night, Sin's going home with me.

Sin had no thoughts. She was just into the sex. She was enjoying Dex wide tongue licks, but was craving for his dick.

"C'mon y'all, lets switch positions," she suggested. Dex nor Flower protested.

Dex somewhat limp, lay on the bed. His thoughts of Flower had mentally turned him off. If he wasn't interested in Sin, this sexual session would've been ended. Just then, Sin crept up licking on Dex's balls, sopping up any wetness Flower left behind. If Dex ever had a case of erectile dysfunction, it was just resolved. His compass meter pointed north, straight into the sky.

"Eeww... looks like somebody's happy to see me," Sin smiled.

"Happy to see you, feel you and get up in you," returned Dex, pulling Sin on top of him.

Flower tried to disguise her attitude. "Can I get in where I fit in? Or is three a crowd?"

"It's never a crowd when it comes to you Flower," replied Sin. "You're always welcomed in my triangle of love. Mount Dex's big ol' juicy lips. I'ma see if I can melt his popsicle stick back here," stirring the head of his dick around her vaginal lips.

Nasty D!ck

Dex couldn't take it no more. Sin's sexual tease was driving him crazy. He eagerly thrust his hips inside of her.

Flower climbed on Dex chest, positioning her pink up against his chin. She couldn't see his facial expressions, but Dex was frowning. *Big ol' pussy, just all in my face.*

His attitude quickly changed when he felt her warm tongue careen against his dick.

Oh... this freak gon' make me cum, thought Dex, moaning and cramping up like he was taking his last breath. Simultaneously being fucked and sucked was an indescribably great feeling.

Sin on the other end was screaming like she'd been shot, gasping from the feeling. Every time she slid downward on Dex's pole, her clit landed on Flower's tongue. Flower was grinding her hips on Dex's tongue as well as glazing his face, neck and chest with her cum.

The trio was having a sexual ball. The eight other women now fully dressed were exiting the room. Already compensated for their job, they figure why continue to be all hot and bothered watching others have fun.

Suddenly, Sin began shaking as if she'd been stamped with a hot branding stick.

"Eeww... I'm cumin'! Pump me Dex! Pump me!" Dex attempted to pump Sin but was frozen with his own climatic high. He lay stiff like a corpse, drained, out of energy as Flower continuously smashed her ass in his face. For the third time, her body juice distilled between the folds of Dex lips, seeping inside his mouth, onto his tongue, sampling her irrigation of ecstasy.

Dex returned home sluggish and tired. He dragged himself upstairs to his bedroom. When he closed the door, he was punched across the mouth. *Whap!*

Dex

The hit dazed him only to be followed up by another blow. *Whap!*

The room was so dark, Dex couldn't see his attacker. He was then thrown over his bed into his dresser with a great crash.

"What the hell was that!" said Barbara awakened from a dead sleep.

"Get up muthafucka! Get yo' ass up!"

Dex wobbly stood onto his feet.

A hand tightly gripped his face.

"Dex, do I look like a bitch to you or something, huh? Do I remind you of one of them females you're fuckin'? Answer me!"

Dex couldn't see the perpetrators face but he did recognize the voice, it was Coke.

Dex nodded, *No* to the question asked.

"Well, that's how you're playing me. You took another $15,000 of my bread, and ain't said shit. That's not your money to spend until the job is done. You're fuckin' up."

"I know Coke. You see..."

Boom! Boom! Boom! "Dexter! Dexter! What's going on in there?" frantically questioned Barbara turning the locked doorknob. "You open this door, right now! Do you hear me?"

Coke pointed his finger in Dex face as a warning, standing off to the side of the bedroom door.

Dex turned on the lights, opening the door.

"Ma! What's the matter?" he yawned standing in the doorway.

Barbara gave him the evil eye. "Dex, it's three in the morning. I'm not up for your games tonight. Now what was that loud noise I heard, and who do you have in that room?" she pointed.

"Nobody Ma. The lights were off and I tripped over something and fell into my dresser. That's what you heard."

"No, I heard voices coming out of here. Who do you got in my house?"

Dex shook his head. "Nobody Ma, honestly. I wouldn't disrespect your house like that."

Barbara folded her arms shifting her weight onto her hip. *I'm sick of this boy; tryin' to convince me I didn't hear what I know I heard,* twisting her lips.

It was more than evident to Dex that his mother had grown weary of him. But whatever he had to say, or however he had to convince her, he was set on not letting his mother in that room. Dex then peered out the corner of his eyes to Coke, who was eyeing Barbara through the crack in the rear of the door.

Keep her talking, Coke indicated with a nod.

Dex looked back to his mother. His shifting eyes were more than enough to confirm Barbara's suspicion. Without warning, she rushed the door, squeezing her body partially in but Dex foot planted behind the door prevented her full entry. Coke immediately hit the lights.

"Let me in!" demanded Barbara pinned by the door. "You're crushing me!"

"Get the hell out then. I told your ass ain't nobody in here!" said Dex trying to push his mother out the room by her face.

"Get your damn hand off my face, Dex! I'm your mother! That's disrespectful!"

Barbara continuously pushed the door with all of her might, exhausting herself. Her wind was at a lost. The pressure from the door was becoming detrimental. She tried

Dex

to utter the words, *I can't breathe,* but the words were caught between her teeth. Because of the darkness, Dex couldn't see his mother losing consciousness. He continued pressing the door with what he'd considered light pressure. As Barbara's last line of defense, she bit into Dex hand.

"Uuuggghhh..!" he screamed trying to shake his hand free, but her lock was fierce, hard and tight like a pit-bull.

"Please momma! Stop! Let go! Please..." pushing the door harder.

Right then, Coke stepped in. He dropped his shoulder and began ramming the bedroom door like a linebacker. Barbara was being crushed to death. Every blow across her chest seemed to take minutes from her life. She knew one day her day for death was coming, *But not like this; not in my own house, wedged in between a door from suffocation,* she thought.

Barbara's fate was sealed. Dex soon felt the pressure of her teeth release from his hand. Suddenly, her body dropped, crashing to the floor. Dex turned on the lights. He looked to his mother's lifeless body, then to Coke.

Coke shook his head. "You done fucked up bad this time, Dex."

Dex was in a panic. "Oh shit! Momma! Momma!" He dropped down to his knees trying to revive her with C.P.R. It wasn't working. Tears wept down his face. "Coke! She ain't breathing man...! My momma ain't breathing." Coke stood aside unsympathetic for Barbara. He could care less about her untimely death. Besides, with her out of the way, it would allow for he and Dex to merge closer.

Dex dragged his mother up the hallway by her arms into her bedroom where he again performed C.P.R. techniques. Still, there was no response. As his last move of

Nasty D!ck

desperation he splashed water across her face. It was useless Barbara appeared to be gone.

Dex sat on the edge of the bed thinking how quickly this tragic incident unfolded. It was now a decision on who to call first; the police or the paramedics.

"Neither one," voiced Coke standing at Barbara's bedroom door. Dex gave a puzzling glare.

"I know what you're thinking Dex, and I said you're calling neither the police, nor the paramedics. I can't allow you to do that. Your mother's dead man, Barbara's dead. And when there's an accidental death in anyone's home, an investigation follows. And if the police come here and collect this body, you're going down. You don't believe me? Take a look at her back or even her chest."

Dex nervously lifted his mothers robe. An imprint from the door was visible across her chest area.

Dex flung her robe shut in disgust. "Damn!"

"See, just like I told you. And you'll find a similar impression on her back. We're going to have to handle this ourselves. I know Dex. It's a difficult decision to make. Maybe the hardest decision you will ever have to make. But ask yourself, do I really want to do time, and I have choice in the matter? Am I built for a twenty-year sentence that a judge might hand down? I know I ain't!" emphasized Coke. He then examined Dex's injured hand.

"This bite looks nasty. The police would find this suspicious. The forensics would find you guilty. Go ahead in the bathroom and get that hand cleaned up. And then, lets deliver ol' Barbara here to her final resting place."

Dex said nothing. He was too choked up, still distraught over what he'd done to his mother, weeping his way into the bathroom.

Dex

In the bathroom, Dex stood running cold water over his sore hand. He flexed his hand watching as the blood ran down into the sink. While doing so, he looked in the mirror hating what he saw. He growled at his reflection, unable to hold his anger from the pain he felt.

"Uuuhhh... I fucked up... I fucked... up," tightly squeezing his hands.

After another ten minutes of mourning and crying, Dex began to come to grips about the situation.

Ok, my momma's dead and I'm responsible for her death, fighting the stabbing feeling. *But Coke's right. I would be convicted behind this for sure. The wounds on momma's body and this bite injury to my hand looks like no accident. I can see it now, son kills fifty-six year old mother in a violent rage, news at eleven. Fuck... that, I'm with Coke. We're going to have to handle this ourselves.*

Dex, sitting on the bathroom toilet finished wrapping his hand. He suddenly heard a thump sounding like it came from his mother's room.

"Coke, wait until I get in there, don't move her body yet."

"Don't move her body yet? Well, what do you plan on doing with her, Dex? You don't plan on calling the police, or paramedics, so what? Hhmm...? Don't choke on me now son. It sounded like you had it all figured out to me," Barbara said.

Dex fell in between the toilet and the wall. The shock factor was overwhelming. Barbara was alive, but armed with her shotgun pointed in Dex's direction.

"Ma! You're alive!"

"Yeah... I'm still amongst the living, no thanks to you though. If you had it your way, flies, worms, beetles, crickets and maggots would be feasting on my remains. How could you do it Dex? Leave your own mother for dead? As bad as I want to cry, I'm too angry to shed a tear. Now get up! My finger is just itching to blow you away. You're no son of mine anymore! she stated backing out the bathroom door.

Dex couldn't believe it. This was like a bad drama scene out of a movie, except he was in it. He stood with his hands up to his chest. He then slowly walked towards the bathroom door, pausing at the entrance.

"Keep walking," she pointed with the shotgun towards the stairs.

Dex could see it in his mother's eyes; the love for him was no more. That sweet woman who nurtured him through her wound was mentally dead. He wanted to turn around to his mother for a hug. He wanted to beg for her forgiveness and plead his case, but Dex knew any sudden move would send him straight to his maker. The two cold steel barrels laid against his back ensured it.

Damn, my momma done lost trust in me.

After walking to the downstairs, Barbara steered Dex towards the front door.

"Ma! You're putting me out?"

"Dex, I fear you. My first instinct is to kill you. Would you prefer that I walk you down into the basement?" He gave no answer. "Open the door," she ordered.

Dex opened the front door, but then bravely turned towards his mother.

"Ma, I'm sorry, please forgive me. I love you," with sorrow in his heart.

Plain and stiff faced, Barbara laid her shotgun on Dex chest. "Love don't live here anymore son," pushing him out the door, slamming it shut.

Dex

It was now six in the morning. After an hour of sitting at the neighborhood park thinking, Dex grew tired. *I need somewhere to crash for a while.*

Broke with no money, and all his financial resources still at his mother's house, Dex found himself pulling up to his son's mother's house, Cree. Even though Cree was a thirty-year-old party girl who sometimes dodged responsibility, she always had a special place in her heart for Dex. Dex knew this, but Cree's irresponsible ways is what always kept him from committing to her.

Dex looked to the side of the house, noticing Cree's bedroom light was on. *Either her ass just got up, or her ass just got in.*

But he knew Cree didn't wake up before twelve noon on any day. Dex walked onto the porch ready to knock on the door, but something didn't feel right. That spoiled feeling was in his gut. He then inched his way up the side of the house to her bedroom window, and peeked inside.

Cree's legs were up in a v-style position, moaning and digging her nails into her lover's back.

Dex dropped his head and leaned his back up against the house and exhaled. *This shit can't be happening,* hurt by what he'd saw. Even though Dex wasn't in a relationship with Cree and hadn't been in years, it didn't lessen the blow.

With his mouth dry, feeling as if he was having an anxiety attack, he again looked back inside the window. Cree's lover was now stroking in a fast motion, ramming between her legs like she was a field goal post.

Through the dim lights, Dex watched in disgust knowing how good and wet Cree's pussy could be. Suddenly, the man pulled out squeezing the head of his dick.

Nasty D!ck

Cree hurried from her back onto her knees, opening her mouth. "Uuuhhh...!" pleasurably he moaned, firing cum all over her face. Cree licked her lips as if the sticky honey were candy. She then attacked his dick sucking down the rest. *That nasty ass bitch!*

Dex rushed around to the front door. Bam! Bam! Bam! "Cree!" he yelled, kicking it. After a minute or so, Cree afraid peeked through the blinds. To her relief it was Dex.

She opened the door dressed in her robe. "Dex! What is your damn problem? And what are you doing here? It's six in the morning."

Dex forced a grin. "What are you doing up?"

"Uumm..."

"It don't matter Cree, I need somewhere to sleep for a few hours. Can I crash here? I'll be gone by twelve," trying to push past Cree.

"Uh, uh! You not staying here!" defensively blocking his entry. "The last time I saw you Dex was 3 weeks ago. You had a pocket full of money, and between me and my son you spent a combined total of $200, but now that your ass is probably broke, you wanna come hollarin' back. Naw Dex, you can keep it movin'."

Dex was pissed. That excuse was bullshit. He looked at Cree like she was the scum of the earth; like she was shit on a stick. It made him want to spit in her face. He could no longer hold it back.

"Bitch! This ain't about no money. You in there fuckin' and suckin' some muthafucka's dick! He's laid up in your bed right now!"

Cree's eyes widened with shock. But before she could get a word in, Dex rushed her out the way.

Dex

"Awe... Shit!" Cree's lover in the bedroom heard everything. He quickly put on his pants and shirt, slipped on his shoes, and stuffed his underwear in his pocket. He then jumped out the bedroom window just as Dex bust through the bedroom door.

Dex ran to the windowsill, sticking his head out. "You better run muthafucka!" only able to see the man's back, running towards the alley. He afterwards turned towards Cree.

"You ain't shit! My son better not be here and you got some other muthafucka' laid up in the bed."

"No, he's not. He's at my sister's. But if he was, this is my house Dex. You don't pay any bills here!"
Dex continued with his questions, pretending not to notice Cree sliding something under the bed with her foot

"So, who was ol' boy?" he asked, in an investigative tone.

"Just somebody to fuck, you haven't been around."

"That simple huh, just a fuck? Whatever. Do I know him?"

Cree frowned. "No, you don't know him. I know how you feel about that, not that it even matters to me."

"It better matter!" hollered Dex. "I'm still fuckin' you!"

He then got down onto the floor and reached under the bed, retrieving what he discovered to be a wallet. He evil eyed Cree.

"Is this what you were trying to hide from me?"

Cree rolled her eyes. Dex opened the wallet. He saw pieces of papers with females phone numbers on them, including Cree's phone number with five stars next to it. *Trifling bitch!*

Nasty D!ck

He then found $32, which he stuck into his pocket. After further rambling, he ran across an Ohio identification card.

"Ohio?" reading the name. "Donald Chandler. Donald Chandler!" looking at the picture on the card. "This is Duck! You're fuckin' Duck, Cree?" looking at her in disgust. "This is my lil' cousin. That's my family."

Cree felt ashamed, she didn't know what to say. She hunched her shoulders. "I'm sorry Dex. It just happened."

"Fuck that! This ain't just happened, you two planned this shit!"

"No Dex. Honestly, we didn't. Duck called me one day talking about the death of his father, and..."

"Hold up, Duck called you? And you two met where?"

"At your mother's house, on Thanksgiving."

That's right. At my mother's house on Thanksgiving. Dex shook his head. He could say no more. He now remembered how he sat with Duck telling him how good Cree was sexually, and how wet she could get. He also thought back to how Duck was starring at Cree's ass the whole night, constantly telling Dex, *'You're a lucky man'.* But Dex didn't think in a million years, Duck; his ninteen-year-old kid cousin would have a shot at his son's mother. *This goes to show you. Don't discuss your woman's sexual skills with no man."*

Dex now felt somewhat responsible. He knew the dogmatic history of the men in his family, he was one of them. Still, he held Cree responsible for her actions.

"Listen Cree, I want you to cut all communication with that lil' muthafucka', you hear me? Duck's ninteen, what can he do for you?"

Dex

"Nothing at all," Cree shook her head thinking, *Nothing but, fuck the shit out of me, until I beg him to suck his dick.*

"Duck only had $32 in his pocket," Dex emphasized. "And you bitchin' at me about only giving you $200? I'll tell you what, I'ma give you a fuck up pass this time Cree. But if it happens again, it's gon' be hell to pay. You understand me?"

Cree nodded.

Dex then went and laid in his son's bed, strategizing and thinking of a plan on how to get the money in his mother's house, out of the basement.

Nasty D!ck

Guilty Conscious

Two days later, Freddy met with Coke. He informed Coke that it had been almost a month since it was thought Ahbicdee had gone to the police. Since that time, Freddy had a change of heart and tried to convince Coke his wife was not a threat to them, or the I.A.A. (International Adoption Agency). He further stated, the hit on his wife's life, should be cancelled. Coke verbally bashed Freddy. He said advance payment for Ahbicdee's demise had already been made, and it was non-negotiable to cancel her hit. Coke went on to explain that Ahbicdee was a greater threat than ever, and told Freddy not to be so easily fooled. Because it had been a month, Ahbicdee more than likely was already an informant for the police, gathering incriminating evidence on him and the agency. Freddy took a moment to think. He knew what was being told to him was possibly true. He also knew that Coke could convince you, a duck could pull a truck if you believed. Freddy argued different.

"Fuck it then!" Coke voiced tired of talking. "Take up your argument with Ock."

Freddy got quiet.

Dex

"That's what I thought. Freddy, I promise you this situation will come to a head. It took some persuasion, but Dex is ready now. He and I will be waiting at our agreed location for Ahbicdee. You just get that Ché broad to play her part like you said, and we will take care of the rest. Are we understood?"

Freddy's lips trembled together, desperately thinking of some type of plea agreement. Coke aggressively repeated himself. "Are we understood?"

Freddy mumbled. "Yes Coke, we're understood."

"Good... And Freddy, don't attempt to act out that story line you got playing in your head, because I'll rewrite the ending. You got me?"

Freddy didn't take kindly to the threat, but nodded his understanding. He then called Ché putting his wife's murder plan into affect.

****

"You haven't said one word since we got into this car. Is everything alright? Answer me Ché. And where are we going?" asked Ahbicdee.

Ché's eyes turned bloodshot red. Her cheeks puffed, as her lips quivered. She quickly pulled to the side of the road, throwing the care into park. She unleashed her tears as she lay upon the steering wheel.

Ahbicdee caressed her back.

"Ché what's wrong. You can talk to me. I'm here for you as you've been there for me. Please Ché, it hurts me to see you this way," she spoke, becoming emotional herself.

Ché leaned back in her seat and took a deep breath. She then looked deep into Ahbicdee's tear glazed eyes. Ché could see her friend had no clue to what was going on. Ché felt the need to alarm her childhood friend and tell her the truth.

I'm in love with Freddy, but regardless of my love for him, I'm not going to let Ahbicdee go out like this.

Ché held Ahbicdee's hand. "I'm sorry that I've been acting so strange. I'm just an emotional wreck right now. But Ahbicdee, I want you to tell me that you forgive me."

Ahbicdee wiped her tears, puzzled.

"Forgive you? Forgive you for what?"

Ché squeezed Ahbicdee's hand harder.

"Please, just do this for me."

"Ok, Ché I forgive you. But what is this about?"

Ché again took a deep breath. She then mustered up some courage.

"Ahbicdee, I'm pregnant, two months pregnant."

"Really! Oh my God. That's wonderful news Ché. Congratulations!"

Ahbicdee overjoyed by the news tightly hugged Ché. "I can't believe this. I'ma be an auntie. Freddy's going to be so happy for you too."

Ché's smiles went dead. Her blue skies turned black. The reality of who her unborn child's father was struck like lightning.

"So... who's the baby's daddy?" asked Ahbicdee walking her fingers like itsy bitsy spider.

Ché slapped her hand. *Don't act dumb bitch! You know Freddy's the father! You know we've been fuckin' around. And you know I'm in love with him!* she screamed in her mind. But Ché's lips spoke a lie.

"Uuhh... I don't think you know the father. His name is Duke. Do you remember him?"

Ahbicdee thought. *Duke? Duke?* "Duke from where? I don't remember no Duke, Ché."

Dex

Shit, I don't either, thought Ché. "He's from some years back, you two will eventually meet," brushing it off. Ché then shifted the car back into drive and took off.

Ahbicdee was smiling from ear to ear.

"Uncle Freddy and Auntie Ahbicdee. That has a nice ring to it, huh Ché?"

Ché nodded with ill thoughts. *More like daddy Freddy, and Ahbicdee out the picture.*

Ahbicdee then sighed. "I don't know, Freddy and I talked a few times about having kids, but it just never happened. And as freaky as that man is, you would've figured me to have at least three or four kids by now."

Sickened by the thought, "It'll happen girl, just give it time," voiced Ché.

"I don't know Ché. I think I'm falling out of love with Freddy. We've been sort of trying to patch our relationship back together, and things are going fine, but for me, it's just not the same. That child abduction thing Freddy was doing has really has curved my heart for him. I don't see him in the same light anymore. Before, that man could do no wrong regardless of what I saw with my own two eyes. But now, I can see that dark streak in him, that side of him that has no remorse for human life. It makes me cold."

"Well, if you feel that way then Ahbicdee, just leave. Why stay?"

"I don't think Freddy will make it that easy for me. We are still married."

"True, but that's all you are, just married. It's not like you two have children bonding you together. You can jet out of there anytime you're ready. Girl, you just need to meet someone you like, and who likes you the same in return. But remember, the next man you give your heart to, make sure he's the man that will take care of your heart."

"I hear you Ché and that's why I love you girl. You're a dear friend who speaks the truth and keeps me out of harms way."

Ché hunched her shoulders. "I do what I can."

****

Dex and Coke were at Ballies Fitness Center. Coke watched as Dex struggled to bench press 225 pounds. After the successful but weary attempt, Dex stood slightly dizzy.

"I didn't come here for this shit," stretching his sore arms. He looked to Coke. "Where's the girl?"

"The girl should be here any minute," repeated Coke for the third time glancing outside the gym's glass windows.

"Any minute, huh? Tell me anything."

Coke held his hands to the side. "What does that mean?"

"It means you're full of shit," throwing his hand. "You claim to have my back, but you ran out on me. You didn't warn me or nothing."

Coke chuckled. "A man... I'm sorry. But that was a big ass gun your momma had. Besides, people at that age don't get charged with murder. They call it justifiable homicide."

Dex squint his eyebrows. "Yeah, and you left me to be the victim. For real, I can still picture that night. My momma would've killed me."

"Relax Dex, calm down. I'll make it up to you. But what we need to do is figure a plan to get that 80 grand out of your momma's house. Any suggestions?"

"Hell naw! Do you have any suggestions?"

"Hell yeah! You have to go back into that house and get that money."

Dex

Dex frowned. "Why you can't do it?"

Coke gave a sinister stare. "Dex, do you honestly want me to retrieve the money? The outcome for your mother won't be pretty."

Dex changed the subject. "So, you're gonna pay me ten thousand more after I do this thing for you, right?"

"Correct."

"And I get Freddy's job too, right?"

"For sho'. You got that," he assured.

The pair afterwards strolled over to the pull-up bars. Dex did five pull-ups before exhausting himself. He sat on the floor. Coke sat next to him.

"So tell me Dex. What did you spend $20,000 on? Seriously."

Dex didn't want to answer the question. The truth made him feel foolish.

"Nothing really," down-playing the answer.

"Nothing really, like what?" asked Coke digging for more.

Dex was irked by the persistence.

"I spent $4000 on clothes, some on my kids and the rest on other lil' shit, you know."

"Ok, and the rest?"

Damn, is Coke my daddy or something? "The rest on uh... p..sy," he mumbled.

"Huh? I didn't hear you, could you repeat that for me?" asked Coke hoping he'd heard wrong.

"Pussy! I said pussy Coke. I tricked the money off, ok?"

Pussy? he thought, shaking his head in disappointment. "Damn...! What kind of pussy was this that cost you 15 grand? Was it a super pussy with a cape hanging out of it? Was it a pussy trimmed in gold with the platinum insides? Or was it some type of investment pussy with a high interest return?"

Dex closed his eyes, shaking his head.

"Naw, none of that; just got caught up with this bitch and her freaky girlfriend who knows how to work a brother's pockets."

"Mmph, this story reminds me of some shit I heard about that tramp you were dealing with years ago; Freddy's ex-wife, Flower."

Dex glanced at Coke. Coke eyed him back.

"Dex! Don't tell me... Flower?"

Dex twisted his lips, turning his head.

"See there, I told you years ago Dex, Flower ain't the one for you. I did hear that her sex game was vicious though, but I also heard that her mentality is scandalous."

"Oh yeah? How so?"

Coke began to explain to Dex how Flower had again remarried some years after she and Freddy's divorce. She took vows with a mature, laid back gentleman named June, who was twenty-four years older than she. June was an old school numbers bookie, who trusted no woman except his twenty year-old daughter, Samantha. But as the years rolled by and June saw more of Flower in numerous locations, she became the prize in his eyes, and he proposed.

After the wedding, June catered and treated Flower like a princess. He bought her a new house, a new car, and a multitude of expensive fur coats and rings, and always proclaimed his love for her. He took her on several trips to exotic islands, even on a safari hunt in Africa. Financially for Flower, June was heaven sent. But sexually, he was a nightmare disaster. June most times was mentally up to the challenge for sex, but physically, he couldn't meet the demand, often leaving his thirty year old Flower frustrated which in turn frustrated him.

June used Viagra, Cialis, and other numerous male stimulants to lift him for the occasion. He even had a penis pump to assist in meeting the needs of his sweetie's uncontrollable desire for sex. But mentally and emotionally, Flower's love for June was dead, often leaving her desert dry. It also didn't help that her husband shunned anal sex in which she loved.

One day, June secretly phoned a male escort service hiring one of their prostitutes. When the young twenty-five year old man arrived, June answered the door shirtless. The escort immediately began to walk away saying he wasn't into satisfying the needs of homosexuals. June quickly told the young man the service was for his wife who was asleep in their bed. June stated. "I only want to watch."

The escort had an issue with that, but the $350 offer persuaded his decision.

After two minutes, the escort nicknamed *Four Play* was ass-naked standing at the foot of the bed. He slowly peeled the warm covers away from Flower's nude body. *She's fuckin' beautiful,* laying eyes on her coco brown skin.

Four Play then crept onto the bed between Flower's legs. He slid one of her legs onto her foot getting a better view of that vaginal slit. Afterwards, he began softly kissing in, out and around Flower's thighs. She was into a dead sleep unaware of a thing, after drinking a whole bottle of White Merlot. June sat in the shadows watching with his arms folded and his legs crossed. His eyebrows were pointing inward. It was difficult to watch another man kissing all over his wife. Suddenly, "Mmm...Mmm... June baby...," moaned Flower.

Nasty D!ck

June sat straight up in his chair somewhat intrigued. It had been a long time since his wife uttered his name in that manner.

Right then, Four Play lift Flower's other leg onto her foot. Her legs were now open. He inhaled the sweet aroma of her vaginal pie, ready to sample a slice. But he instead steered his tongue two inches lower exploring the brown-eye express. Flower screamed on contact, gripping the sheets. She arched her back as if she'd been possessed by an omen. After giving into the tongue-lashing dream inside of her ass, she began to relax. She started caressing Four Play's baldhead grinding her hips along with the motion of his tongue. Four Play could see the slimy wetness oozing from the slit of her pussy. His nine-inch dick became harder. He then rolled on his rubber and laid on top of Flower. That's when June stood up. Even though he enjoyed how his wife was passionately calling his name, and he was the one who contacted the escort service, this other man thing was fucking with him. But this situation for him had reason, so he let it continue.

Four Play spread Flower's legs wide open, holding them over his shoulders. He pushed himself inside. "Mmm...!" she moaned, feeling the dick scrape the back of her wall.

After that single thrust, Flower began to realize this was no dream. She reached around feeling the tight, smooth feeling of Four Play's balls, unlike the saggy, hanging nuts of her husband, June. Flower then opened her eyes. Because of the wine consumption, it took her a minute to bring her eyes into focus.

"What the fuck!" eyeing the stranger on top and inside of her. "Get the fuck off of me!" she shoved, savoring

Dex

the feeling of that good, hard dick exiting her pussy. "Who are you? How did...?"

"Baby, baby. Calm down," said June rushing to her bedside.

"June?" Flower questioned.

"Yeah baby. You know you and I have been having this sexual problem thing so I called Four Play here in to give you a little satisfaction. But if you don't want him here, I understand baby," rubbing his wife's shoulder, hoping she would dismiss the escort.

Flower clearly understood what was going on, but still she pretended to be distraught by her awakening.

She rubbed her fingers through the beast like hairs on June's chest. "Daddy, you didn't have to do that for me. It's you and your dick that I love," she lied.

That's the answer June was searching for.

"Ok bro, your services are no longer needed," handing Four Play $350.

Four Play's dick went limp. Not to finish the job was a big disappointment for him. He could tell from Flower's wetness, she was just getting into the sex.

Flower felt some disappointment too. Even though she was half sleep that was the best dick she had since being married. She watched as Four Play was pulling up his pants. She couldn't take her eyes off that cannon between his legs. That hunk of pipe soon disappeared behind his zipper.

"Stop! I mean... hold on," Flower pointed to Four Play. She then directed June to the next room.

"Baby..." she dragged with puppy dog eyes. "Since the escort is here and you already paid him, would you mind if he finished."

June felt his legs giving out from underneath him. He felt his throat along with his mouth getting dry. It was breaking his heart to know his princess desired another man's love. "Is that...? I mean... if that's what you want," he stuttered to say.

"You do want me to be satisfied, don't you daddy?"

"Yeah... But... I thought..."

Flower cut him short.

"Then, I want you to come join in baby. I'ma fuck you and suck you so... good," licking and sucking his earlobe.

June caught the chills. He gave his approval. Before long, Four Play was ramming his package inside of Flower's mailbox. He was giving it to her long and hard, almost bringing his dick completely out the pussy before crushing her walls all over again.

June standing in the next room naked could hear the sounds of sex. The bed was beating against the wall. He couldn't believe what he was allowing to go on in his house, with his own wife. In one way he felt ashamed. In another, it was anger.

"Why can't I be the one in there giving my wife mad sex?" wishing for younger days. He fought back the tears he wanted to shed. "I love my wife," he told himself. He then stepped into the room.

June watched as Four Play's thighs repeatedly slap against his wife's ass, imagining it were himself. Flower's ass sting and her pussy throbbed, but she welcomed it all, opening her mouth tasting the sweat that ran off of his face. "Mmm... Ewww..." loving the hardness of his dick.

Just then Four Play flipped Flower out the bed onto the floor. She could feel the rug burn into her back from every thrust he took. She was sucking his fingers, as he held his hand over her mouth, fucking the shit out of her, listening to her groan as if she was being raped.

Dex

Flower on her back looked up at Four Play. *Oh God, I don't even remember this man's name. But he's giving it to me like he's making love. Make me wanna pull that rubber off and have his baby.*

Flower then looked to June who had his dick in his hand, approaching to get in and make this a threesome. She rolled her eyes.

Uh...! I can't stand June's old ass and them grey hairy balls of his. Get on my nerves; always trying to stick that fake feeling dick up in somebody. It doesn't even feel real. The only thing June can do for me is give me some money. But the way this boy is beatin' up in this pussy, just made me realize, I want out of my marriage.

June approached, but before he even spoke a word, Flower shut him down.

"Baby..." she moaned. "I'ma call on you when I'm ready for you. Just keep it hard for me, ok daddy?"

June backed off. He again watched standing in the shadows. Flower was bent over with her face lying on her hands. Four Play's hips were moving double time, slapping the side of her ass. Her love canal moistened from every stroke. June could hear the soaking wet, juicy sounds her pussy was making. He was now envious never recalling himself bringing his wife to such a peak. For the second time June tried to join in. Flower again, rejected him.

Four Play intervened. "Pops, please... Let me handle this. Take a seat on the bed, and your wife will call you as soon as she's ready for you. Remember now, keep it hard for her daddy." Flower giggled.

Pops, huh? thought June. *Ok.* He left out of the room. Four Play continued laying down his skills. He inserted two fingers inside of Flower's ass, at the same time, popping her coochie. She began going wild having sexual convulsions.

Nasty D!ck

Four Play then squeezed her titties. Flower screamed. An atomic eruption of cum exploded down her thighs, leaking onto Four Play's balls. He too skeet a snowfall of cum between the crack of her ass after sliding off his rubber. The loud sexually intense breathing soon began to come to a rest. "Welcome to satisfaction," said Four Play trying to catch his breath.

Suddenly, out of nowhere. Bop! Bop!

Four Play's bottom teeth went flying. He fell to the floor, holding his mouth.

"What are you doing!" Flower yelled to June who had a pistol in his hand.

"Call me pops, huh? Disrespect me in my own house! I'aint cha damn daddy," standing over Four Play who was curled in a ball.

After pistol-whipping Four Play, June drug him outside naked onto the front porch, where he left him. June soon returned to give Flower a beating, sticking his pistol into her mouth.

"You wanna suck on something? Huh! Well suck on this bitch!" making Flower put her mouth around the pistol. He then ordered her to lick around the barrel of the gun as if it were a dick. "Pretend it's me," grimming with a deranged stare.

Flower felt humiliated. She felt scared. Tears spilled down her face. She couldn't believe June was doing this to her. She was just about to make a plea for her life when suddenly, June regained his sanity realizing what he was doing. He dropped his gun and broke down into tears.

"Oh God! Lord, Jesus! I'm so sorry!"

He crawled up to Flower, holding her waistline, begging for her forgiveness. Flower saw this as an opportunity for her to get out. A way she could legitimately

Dex

be done with this miserable marriage. But she knew June would never let her go that easy. He loved her too much to let her go; to a point where he might would kill her. Fearing for her life, Flower gave her forgiveness.

One night, six months after that episode, June returned home. He tried his house keys in the front and back doors. It was strange, they all seemed not to work. He began to beat on the front door and knock on the windows. There was no answer. He figured the loud music coming from inside the house was drowning out his knocks.

After thirty minutes of sitting on the front porch, June grew tired. "Fuck this."

He went around to the bathroom window and pried it open. He climbed halfway through the window when, Boom! Boom! Boom!

June was struck once in the head and twice in the back. He fell dead inside the bathtub where his blood leaked down into the drain.

"Damn! So Flower killed June?" asked Dex feeling stunned.

"Hell yeah, and with the same gun he pulled on her six months ago," responded Coke. "Flower told the police she thought her husband was a burglar. The question of why June entered his own house through the bathroom window to this day is still a mystery. But what no one knew is, Flower secretly had the door locks changed around the house that day. So, after she killed June, she took his old house keys from his key ring and put the new ones on, and then slipped the keys back into his pocket. It was the perfect murder plan. She took $200,000 from the safe and she received another $100,000 from the insurance company on an accidental death policy, he'd taken out on himself years ago. June figured that one day he possibly would be killed in the street collecting his money, not by his own wife."

"Man...that's fucked up! It took some precision planning to think up some shit like that. You called it Coke, Flower's scandalous."

"Yeah, but hold up. That's a fraction of it. Do you know who's June's daughter Samantha is?"

Dex couldn't figure it out. "No."

"Well, Flower, and June's daughter Samantha became a couple after his death. So, whoever Flower's hooked up with now, that's June's daughter."

It didn't take him long.

"Sin!" Dex frowned, hit with another blow.

"If that's her name, then that's her. You'd better watch those bitches Dex. I told you, Coke has your back."

Dex was fucked up behind the story Coke had just told him. *I knew Flower wasn't right, I could see it in her eyes. But Sin, I didn't see that one coming. Help set her own daddy up? Boy, that's some shit to think about. And I was digging her too. All those nuts I bust in her. I just hope this broad ain't pregnant.*

Just then, Coke pointed towards the gym's check-in counter. "There's the girl over there now," recognizing Ché from Freddy's home porno video.

Dex looked. He saw three females standing at the counter unsure of which one was the intended target. "You see her right, Dex?" asked Coke.

"Mmm... mmph. Yeah," Dex confirmed, starring at one of the women in a trance like state. He couldn't take his eyes off of this woman. She was beautiful; a heavenly creature. Dex felt weird. He felt like he was already catching feelings, like he was in love.

Dex

"Dex!" Coke whispered for the fourth time. "Wake the fuck up! I said they're headed this way," stepping aside. Dex snapped out of it.

"Uh... Oh, I'm on it. I'm on it. Don't worry. I got this."

Ahbicdee, Ché and the woman they were conversing with at the counter, were all approaching. Dex stood in their path rehearsing his signal line that would inform Ché of who he was. As the women neared, Dex and the heartthrob woman he was starring at made eye contact. Dex's heart skipped a beat, which caused him to lose his breath. The trio then passed him by entering the aerobic class.

Coke walked back up. "What the hell was that? Why didn't you give the signal? All you have to say is, 'Hi, I'm Dex' and the rest is done. The girl, Ché knows the drill. Get your ass in there and give that signal. This is no time to catch cold feet on me now, Dex."

Coke was laying the pressure on thick. He wanted Ahbicdee dead. He figured he'd went through too much trouble putting this thing together to let Dex fuck it up now.

Dex had fun spending the twenty grand, but he could now see it came with a price. He could see Coke wasn't playing any games, and was serious about this murder. *What have I've gotten myself into?* he sighed.

Dex was approaching the entry door of the aerobics class when he looked back at Coke. Coke was fiercely waiving his hand at Dex, as to say, *Get your ass in there!* Dex walked in.

Inside the aerobics class, most of the participates were women, with the exception of one other man. Dex put his hand over his mouth smiling.

Oh shit! Pussy jackpot! looking at all the panty lines and the asscheeks bulging through the spandex pants. He

119

hawk-eyed through the crowded room of women as they placed their foot-steppers in front of them. The class was ready to start when the aerobic trainer suddenly looked to Dex who was standing at the door.

"Well, are you going to step along with all of these lovely ladies, or are you just going to stand there and drool?" The women laughed. Dex turned around, then looked back. "Who me?" pointing to himself.

"Yes you. Come on in. Get your heart rate up," she encouraged.

Dex tried to shy away, but all those fine women waving him inside was undeniable. He grabbed a foot-stepper. Before long, he was five minutes into the workout session and felt like his was dying. Sweat was pouring from his face. His arms and thighs were burning. He was exhausted. Every minute that passed made him want to call it quits.

I didn't come her for this shit, marching up and down and around the foot-stepper.

Dex head nodded to the other gentleman in the room who wasn't missing a beat. He afterwards glanced over his shoulder at Ahbicdee, Ché and a few others. They too appeared to be having the time of their lives. But Dex felt like he had nothing more left in himself. After another agonizing twenty minutes, *I can't take no more,* breathing hard, off balance, and ready to quit.

"And stop!" said the aerobics trainer as the techno music came to an end. "Ok, ladies, and gentlemen, that was great. Greet and say hello to your workout neighbor, and we'll all see each other next time."

Some workout participants left, most stayed. Dex realized he had a good time after he caught his breath. Feeling the rush of the exercise session, he'd forgotten what

Dex

he'd come in there for. He made it his duty to meet some of the ladies around the room.

"Hi, I'm Dex," he spoke shaking hands with several of the women. "Hi, what's your name sweetie? Veronica? Hi, Veronica, I'm Dex," shaking her hand.

The greetings were repetitious and quick. So quick, Dex didn't realize the person he was greeting next was the woman he had his eye on, the woman that would change his life forever. He reached for her hand, glaring into her voluptuous eyes. Dex was mesmerized by her beauty. His mind suddenly traveled in thought.

As you stand before, me I announce my love
There's no mistaking in my heart, I know you're the one
I just wanna hold your hand and look into your eyes
Actions are louder than words, they speak no lies
Don't wanna run you off by tellin' you how fine you look
But when I first saw you girl, my world was shook
And it's much too soon to be talkin' 'bout sex
But the mental connection caused me to become erect
I'm sorry love, didn't mean to come at you like that
But let me tell you about my life, let me drop a few facts
I'm Dex, 35, got some whorish ways
Since I was 16 years old, I've had this sexual craze
One woman for me, just wasn't enough
I picked them like bananas, I gathered a bunch
I did what I did, then threw them to the side
Didn't catch no feelings, just continued to ride
Didn't love them hoes, oops... I mean the ladies
Behind all that screwing, I kicked out seven babies
Couldn't roll against the grain, it was the way I was raised
But now that I've met you, hoping to change my ways
I think I love you baby, don't wanna rush you too fast

Nasty D!ck

I think I love you baby, this ain't about no ass
This about you and me, on a whole 'nother level
You only live once, take a chance with this fellow
I can see you're scared, you've been hurt before
But if you follow my lead, you will hurt no more
Let me walk you through the field, I mean the green grass
I got some money put away, 'bout a 80 grand stash
Just wanna wine you, dine you, be the man in your life
Spend the weekend in Vegas, I wanna spoil my wife
But it's all on you, you have to make the first step
Spending your life with me, you won't have no regrets

"What are your names again sweetie?"

"This is Ché, my best friend, and my name is Ahbicdee."

"Hi Ché and Ahbicdee, I'm Dex."

Ché's smile went stiff. Her eyes widened to the whites. *It's him!* She suddenly bent over holding her stomach. "Oh... Oh..." she moaned.

Ché! Are you okay?" urgently asked Ahbicdee, assisting her friend down onto the floor. She looked to the instructor. "She's pregnant! Call a doctor! Just hold on girl, paramedics will be here any minute," rubbing Ché's hand.

The women in the room huddled in a circle around Ché, handing her bottles of water. Ché was taking short breaths trying to catch her wind.

"I'm... I'm... ok," she insisted trying to get up.

Ahbicdee wasn't hearing it.

"Naw, naw. You just hold on right here until the ambulance arrives. Don't want to take any chances on you losing my niece or nephew there in your stomach," cupping the back of her head. "I told you, you've been there for me, now I'm here for you."

Dex

Ché smiled but she felt like shit on the inside. Here her best friend Ahbicdee was showing the deepest concern for her well being, and Ché brought her there to meet the contract hit man who was hired to murder her, which caused Ché to panic when she heard the signal, realizing Dex was the hired killer. She could only think, *There's no turning back now.*

Dex stuck his head in through the crowd of women. "Paramedics are on their way. Is there anything else I can do to help?" looking down to Ché on the floor. Ché turned her head to the side.

"No, you've done enough," spoke Ahbicdee, again shaking Dex hand pulling him aside.

Dex looked deep into Ahbicdee's eyes.

Damn, so this is Ahbicdee? Freddy's wife? The one he wants dead? The one that Coke wants dead? The woman I've been hired to kill? The woman that has stolen my heart? What could she possibly have done to deserve such a fate?

Hello... Hello," said Ahbicdee, snapping her fingers in Dex's face. "Are you there?"

"I'm sorry Ahbicdee, it's just...," Dex paused, still holding her hand.

"It's just what?"

"That you're so beautiful. Not to come off on you corny or anything, but you are."

Ahbicdee blushed. "Thank you Dex. I needed that."

"It's the truth. But say my name again. I like the way it sounds coming off your lips."

"What? Dex?"

"Yeah baby, that's it. I'ma have to keep you close to me, have you saying it day and night."

Nasty D!ck

Ahbicdee put up her left hand, displaying her wedding band. Dex covered her ring finger with his hand.

"That means nothing if you're not happy."

Ahbicdee looked towards the floor knowing it was the truth. Dex wasn't searching for Ahbicdee's vulnerable side but he found it in a general conversation.

Awe, man... that was too easy. Ahbicdee is standing strong before me but she's really hurtin'. What has she been through? Mmph, if Freddy's still half the son of a bitch he was years ago, and I know he's three times that now, then this woman has been fucked over. And I'm just on time to pick up the pieces.

Ahbicdee was into her own thoughts. *Ahbicdee! Girl... quit letting yourself be so easily read. So what you're no longer happy in your marriage, you don't have to let the whole world know it. But this guy Dex seems pretty nice. He's handsome too. And his conversation is on point. I wonder... No, no Ahbicdee. You're married, faithfully married. But what the hell does that mean? Freddy isn't to me.* She then spoke. "Dex, would you maybe, sometime soon like to grab a cup of coffee?"

Dex laughed. "A cup of coffee, huh? I can tell you don't do this very often."

Ahbicdee again put up her hand. "Married," thinking, *Did you forget?*

"Oh, that again," Dex threw his hand, thinking, *That's nothing.* He leaned in towards her ear.

"After that cup of coffee, whoever he is, be ready to give him back that ring."

Chills ran down Ahbicdee's spine. She closed her eyes as her panties moistened. It wasn't what Dex said that turned her on but the heat of his breath on her neck. It had been quite sometime since she'd felt like this.

Dex

I guess Ché was right. I just needed to meet someone I liked, who in return liked me the same, and it appears I found that likeness in Dex.

Ché still on the floor watched as Ahbicdee smirked and giggled from Dex's every word. The way he held her hand and how she was giving him her undivided attention. Ché didn't want Ahbicdee to go out like this, but if this was the only way she could have Freddy for her own, then so be it. Right then, the paramedics arrived.

"You have a pregnant woman here?" the ambulance driver asked.

"Right here, over here," Ahbicdee pointed towards Ché.

The circle of concerned women dispersed allowing the paramedics to do their job. Soon after, Ché was loaded into the back of the ambulance truck.

Dex and Ahbicdee agreed to meet at the gym the next day. From there they would go and have lunch and that cup of coffee. Dex then waved Ahbicdee and Ché off as they rode away in the ambulance.

Just then, Coke walked up giving Dex that look.

"What?" Dex hunched his shoulders.

"You know damn well what?" barked Coke. "This ain't no love connection here. You're in there holding hands with this woman like she's your bitch. Ahbicdee is Freddy's wife, remember? She's the target. You supposed to meet her, befriend her and kill her. Very simple. How hard is that?"

Coke put his finger one inch from Dex's eye.

"I'll tell you what Dex. If this thing isn't done in a timely matter, or I even suspect you're falling for this broad, which I think you are, then don't worry about the hit. In fact, fuck the twenty grand you owe too. I'll run a knife in Ahbicdee's gut myself."

Nasty D!ck

Afterwards, Coke walked off. *Think I'm playing with his ass!*

Dex

Fucked with the Wrong One

Freddy observing Ahbicdee over the past three weeks began to notice a change in her daily routines. Her everyday phone calls home on her lunch break reduced to just once a week. Her hair, which she usually did herself was now being professionally done every week. New outfits were popping up; new scents of perfume were lingering, and she stayed on the go. When Freddy confronted Ahbicdee about her slight profile change, she stated with an attitude.

"I'm just taking some me time."

Some me time? Freddy thought. He knew better than that. He knew what the situation was, which made him a little jealous.

Dex's supposed to be killing my wife, not fucking my wife. I just know he is, standing with the freezer door open.

"Freddy, is something on your mind? I thought you were going to make us a couple of drinks?" said Renee, Freddy's lady friend sitting on the couch.

"Oh, my fault baby."

Freddy shook and poured the drinks. He then carried the martini glasses over to the couch.

Renee took a gulp of her drink.

"Eeww, that's good." She afterwards slid all three of the green olives from the toothpick into her mouth. "I love olives," downing the rest of her drink. "Make me another," she demanded.

Freddy gave Renee a cold look. *Ol' drunk ass, greedy bitch,* now back in the kitchen making another drink.

As Freddy broke up the ice in the ice trays, the phone rang. He checked the phone's caller ID and squint his eyes. *Damn.*

"Hey..." he answered the line. "What's going on?"

"Freddy! I thought you were calling me back!" snapped Ché. "I told you I wanted to come see you today."

Freddy held the line listening to Ché's complaints. Finally, he heard enough.

"Ché please, stop it with that bullshit! This thing with Ahbicdee isn't even done yet, and it's like you're trying to be with me already. Damn, have some type of respect for your girl."

With that statement made, Ché continued going off. Freddy really not giving a fuck, still continued to hold the line.

Renee who was watching and ear hustling Freddy's conversation was growing impatient.

"Damn, he could've at least brought me my drink before he started talking," ready to leave.

Freddy read the irritation across Renee's face. He put up his finger as to say, *Give me a minute.*

After another five minutes, Renee had enough. She felt disrespected. She twisted her lips, throwing up her middle finger. *Fuck you.*

Freddy placed his palm over the receiver's speaker. "Hold on baby," he begged Renee, putting the phone back to his ear.

Ché got quiet. "You got another bitch over there, don't you? Hell naw! I'm on my way!"

Dex

Freddy hung up the phone. *Wish I would've never fucked that bitch!* rushing over to Renee.

"What's up baby? Where you going? I thought you were going to chill with me," trying to kiss Renee's neck.

She backed him off. "I was Freddy, but you got too many bitches calling here for me. And besides, I just saw a picture of you and your wife laying face down on the mantelpiece. You didn't tell me you were married. So, where is she?"

"Who?"

"What do you mean, who? Your wife, Freddy."

"Shit, she's at work."

Renee snarled her lip and squint her eye.

"Oh, you're a dog," opening the front door.

Freddy slammed the door shut. He stroked his goatee, eyeing the narrow cut in Renee's breast.

"So, you just gon' walk out of here with out giving me some pussy, huh?"

Renee was confused, closing the top button on her shirt. "I beg your pardon. What are you talking about? Listen Freddy, thanks for the drinks but I have somewhere I have to be," again trying to open the front door.

It was useless. Freddy's foot was planted against the door. Then suddenly, he started unbuckling his pants. "Renee, you've got two choices. You can either give me that pussy, or I'ma take that pussy. The choice is yours."

Renee clinched her fists. "Well, I guess you just gon' hafta take it, 'cause I'm not giving up shit."

Without warning, Whap! Freddy slapped the shit out of Renee. Black, blue and white stars swirled her eye sockets. The hit came so fast, she didn't see it coming. Freddy naked, was in a fighters stance.

Nasty D!ck

"Make it easy on yourself bitch! Drop them drawers. You know you want it."

He then tried to rush Renee onto the couch. They fell to the floor. Freddy on top popped every button off her shirt, snatching at her bra, squeezing her titties.

"Get the fuck off of me Freddy!" she screamed, but her requests went ignored.

Freddy had that mad man, kill'a hoe look on his face. He then tightly squeezed her throat.

"I told you bitch! Didn't I tell you? It didn't hafta come to this!" reaching under, snatching her pants down from the crack of her ass.

Please no! Please... Renee's mind spoke. The words were trapped in her throat.

After her pants were off, Freddy mercilessly ripped off her panties. "Give me those!" sniffing the garment's pussy scent. As he did so, Renee saw her opportunity to escape. She gripped Freddy by the thighs and kneed him in the nuts, unfortunately not with enough force. Freddy grit his teeth and again slapped the shit out of Renee.

"Uh...! holding her stinging face. This time she tasted the blood. *Awe shit Renee,* she said to herself weak and tired. *We might not win this fight.*

Freddy's strength seemed to amplify with Renee's every struggle. Before long, his fingers were swimming inside her surprisingly wet pussy.

"Yeah, this bitch like that shit!"

Soon after, Renee's legs were cocked east and west. Freddy entered from the south and began pushing upward towards the north.

"Uh! Uh! Uh!" Freddy emphasized with every thrust he took, pushing deeper inside.

Dex

"You ain't shit! You ain't shit Freddy," moaned Renee, welcoming that hard dick inside her watery hole. She then clamped her feet around his legs and began fucking him back. Freddy palmed her head with one hand and gripped her ass with the other, pulling her body towards his hips, eyeing her wetness on his raw dick.

"Mmm mmph, I see you ain't fighting no more. Love the way that dick feel, don't you?" now stroking her clit with his thumb.

"Yes, baby. You're fucking the shit out of me. Lay down on top of me. Give it to me deeper, harder!"

Deeper and harder, damn she's a freak. But Freddy did as Renee asked. He pushed deeper and harder inside. His toes gripped the carpet. His nuts were slapping against her ass like a standing ovation.

It was everything Renee had imagined rape/sex to be. She felt the assisting muscles in his back. His hot mouth around her neck, and him tapping on the wall of her uterus. Renee rolled her eyes. *This dick is the bomb,* thinking how sore she was going to be the next day.

"C'mon baby, turn over. Let me hit that ass from the back."

"You want some of this juicy pussy from the back? Ok baby," excited about having sex on camera.

As Renee was about turned over, she suddenly started screaming, eyeing the stranger standing behind Freddy.

Freddy on his knees had no idea of what startled Renee. "What the fuck is wrong with you!" trying to calm her down. But that fearful glare across Renee's face told Freddy to look behind himself. He turned around.

"You still shootin' these home porno flicks I see," said Coke picking up Freddy's video camera.

Freddy was relieved, at the same time furious.

131

Nasty D!ck

"Coke, what the fuck man! You can't just be walking up in my shit like this," slipping on his robe. "And you scared the shit outta my girl."

"Better me than Ahbicdee, right?" he chuckled.

Renee was pissed. "This is bullshit Freddy!" pulling up what was left of her panties. "I just know you and your friend here don't think you're about to run a train on me on video. Hell... to the no! Not with this bitch y'all won't," now tying her shoes. She then opened the front door. "The acted out rape scene was fun. The dick was good. It's just too bad I didn't get to cum," walking out, slamming the door.

"Shit, I didn't get to cum either," said Freddy.

"Freddy, you gotta quit bringing those types of females home," lectured Coke.

"Coke, you have to quit breaking into my home period," returned Freddy. "How do you do that anyway?"

Before Coke could answer, Boof! Boof! Boof!, came a hard knock at the front door.

Freddy without looking opened the door thinking it was Renee. Ché stepped in looking Freddy up and down. "Are you fuckin' around on me?" she asked.

Freddy frowned. "What!"

"You heard me! I just saw some bitch pulling away from this house as I was pulling up, and it wasn't Ahbicdee. Was that the bitch I heard over the phone?"

Freddy sighed. "Ahbi... I mean, Ché please."

"Oh, about to call me Ahbicdee, huh?" Ché broke in tears. "Freddy, this whole situation is becoming impossible to deal with. I love you with all my heart and I just can't see myself being without you. You're my world."

Ché then embraced Freddy for a hug. He petted and rubbed her back.

Dex

"Ché, be cool. Relax baby. Give it a minute. This thing is gon' work itself out, I promise," kissing her forehead.

Coke standing in the kitchen didn't like none of what he was hearing. *Freddy doesn't have the power over this Ché broad like he claimed. She's mouthy and too emotional. Therefore, she's a threat.*

Ché laying her head on Freddy's chest looked upward into his eyes. "Did that girl I just saw leave here?"

Freddy stared back with sincerity. "No baby, she didn't"

Ché then unexpectedly reached her hand through the front of Freddy's robe, cupping his dick. He jerked backwards. Ché sniffed her hand. The smell of sex lingered from her palm. Ché hit him in the chest.

"You're a liar! You fucked her!"

Freddy fired back. "And what do you call it that I do with you? You got the game twisted Ché. I don't owe you no excuses for what I do. You're not Ahbicdee. You're just the woman on the side."

That was more than an ear full for Ché. She felt hurt, cut, her heart was bleeding.

Freddy continued. "So now what? What you gon' do, tell Ahbicdee we're all plotting to kill her? Tell the police we're all in a plot to kill my wife? Or, are you going to mention to them that I snatch kids and have them smuggled out of the country, huh? Because if I go down Ché, you're going down with me."

Tears wept down Ché's face. She heard how mean Freddy could be, but didn't know how mean, until now.

"Freddy, I'm no better than you," spoke Ché, holding her head down. "My love for you has made me betray my best friend and will possibly cost me my freedom. But this child of yours I'm carrying will not be poisoned by your treacherous ways."

Freddy almost lost his legs. "Child of mine? You're pregnant?"

"Yes Freddy, I'm pregnant. Don't you worry though, you won't be a part of this child's life. But I am going to tell my friend how dishonest I've been in our friendship. I don't know what will happen behind this Freddy, but Ahbicdee deserves the truth." Ché opened the front door.

"Ché!" Freddy called.

Ché paused for a moment, listening, hoping Freddy would tell her what to do; hoping he'd lend his strength to her broken heart, but he said nothing. She then continued out the door never looking back.

Coke stepped out of the kitchen. "This is not good," shaking his head towards Freddy.

"Well, what do you want me to do Coke? You heard what Ché said. She's carrying my unborn child. This will be my first. This is something Ahbicdee could never give me."

Coke exhaled. He didn't care about Freddy's first unborn child. His thoughts were on how his plan was going out the window, and how the possibility of him being in prison was more than evident. Something had to be done and fast.

"C'mon, throw some clothes on. Lets take a ride," he told Freddy.

"Where are we going?" Freddy suspiciously asked.

"Cut it with all the questions. Just get ready."

Within minutes, Freddy was dressed. After stepping outside, he again asked Coke where were they going. Coke ignored Freddy's question, throwing him the car keys.

"You drive," hopping onto the passenger side.

Dex

Freddy briefly stood with the keys in his hand. He quickly made up an excuse to go back inside the house, but Coke insisted there was no time. Freddy got inside the car appearing to be uneasy. He was hoping this car ride wasn't to be his last.

Coke looked. "Will you start this car and lets go Freddy, looking like you have to shit or something."

As Coke navigated Freddy through the streets to their destination, he eyed the bulge on Freddy's right hip.

This muthafucka' Freddy is armed with a pistol and he's still scared of me. Probably thinking I'm about to take him somewhere and try to kill him. I figured this much, that's why I had him drive. If he wanted to pull his pistol, he couldn't. His weapon is positioned awkwardly on his hip. Shit, I could take his gun if I wanted to, he smirked.

Freddy was nervously watching Coke from the corner of his eye. *What is Coke smirking at? He just doesn't know I'm packing my 45 automatic. He tries anything and I'ma paint the inside of this car with his fucking brains. I really didn't plan on driving, it kind'a puts me in a vulnerable situation. My gun is awkwardly positioned on my right hip. Something tells me Coke already knew that,* continuing his uneasy glare. Within ten minutes, the pair arrived to their destination.

"Pull in here," Coke pointed to the housing complex parking lot.

Freddy pulled up and parked. He pointed. "This is..."

"I know what it is!" Coke cut him short. "Let me borrow this," snatching the 45 from Freddy's hip. He then hopped out of the car, looking back to Freddy. "Watch my back. This will only take a second."

"Coke!" Freddy called. "You can't do this!"

Nasty D!ck

Coke paid him no mind, as he walked up to Barbara's front door with the pistol in his hand like a western gunslinger. He planted his foot in the middle of the front door with all his might. Bam! The door literally came off its hinges, falling to the floor.

Freddy held his hands on his head.

"What the fuck am I doing here?"

In broad daylight, it was hard not to hear the commotion. Some neighbors were looking out of their windows. One old lady who has lived in her home for years, and who knew Barbara well, heard the disturbance and made her way out in front.

After five minutes, Coke emerged out the house with his bag containing the $80,000. Luckily for Barbara, she wasn't home. If she had been and pulled that shotgun on Coke, he was prepared to kill her.

As Coke walked past the old lady, she asked, "Boy, why are you doing this to Ms. Barbara? She took good care of you over the years, and this is how you repay her?

Coke turned towards the old lady.

"Deliver this to Ms. Barbara, with your old ass, if you can see it." He was displaying his middle finger.

The old lady was appalled. Coke then jumped into the car handing Freddy back his 45. The two then burned rubber from the scene.

Later that night, Coke was riding Dex's back about Ahbicdee's murder. He was raging mad and edgy, accusing Dex of prolonging her death because of his feelings for her, which Coke had warned him about. Dex denied those claims, stating Ahbicdee's demise hadn't been met because the opportunity hadn't presented itself. However, he did claim

Dex

within 72 hours Ahbicdee would no longer walk amongst the living. Coke appeared to be at ease from this promising speech, but he didn't believe one word Dex spoke. Coke knew Dex's heart. It wasn't as cold as he wanted Coke to believe. Coke was now prepared to take matters into his own hands.

I told Dex what I was gon' do if he fell for that bitch. I guess I'ma hafta show em' better than I can tell him.

"Dex, lets take a ride," said Coke.

Dex was suspicious. "Take a ride where?"

"Don't ask questions, just come on."

Within 15 minutes the pair were pulling up to the Purple Slip Gentlemen's Club. Dex was confused looking around the parking lot.

"What are we doing here? I'm not trying to see that bitch Flower or Sin."

"What? Do they scare you or something?" asked Coke.

"Hell naw... it's just. It don't matter, lets go."

The two stepped inside the bar. The atmosphere was dim with different colored neon lighting. The laser lights throughout the room were displaying a multitude of patterns along the floor. The baseline from the music was vibrating their chests and the butt naked dancers strolled back and forth. One dancer came by doing a shoulder dance along with shaking her titties. She asked Dex, what did he want to do. He put both his hands to his chest as to say, *Nothing at all.* She then continued on her way.

"You didn't like her? She had an ass on her," said Coke, finding it weird Dex was overlooking these naked women.

"Dime a dozen," commented Dex scanning the bar for Flower and Sin. He didn't see any signs of neither woman, which put him at ease.

"So what are we doing here Coke?"

Coke ignored Dex's question bouncing to the beat, handing Dex a $100. "Order us some drinks and find us a booth."

Dex walked up to a waitress. "Let me get two Cirocs and Cranberry, and... two shots of Patron. I'll be seated in that booth, right there," he pointed up the way.

As Dex walked towards his booth, he rubbernecked other booths to catch some of the action. He saw a dancer bent over the table with the customer's face literally in her ass.

My man is eatin' her pussy! He walked pass the next booth to see another dancer with her leg positioned up over the customer's shoulder. His head was slowly moving back and forth.

Damn, he's her eatin' pussy too!

The next three booths Dex walked by, he saw dick licking, dick riding, and dick sucking. The scenery was so out cold, he couldn't help but to wonder where security was. He then looked towards the far corner of the bar. Security had a couple of dancers of their own showing them a good time. *This some wild shit.*

Dex was focused on his booth just up ahead, when he laid eyes on a gentleman and two other women in a triangle tongue kiss, in the booth next to his. He quickly turned his head trying not to stare. He afterwards sat down at his booth with an uptight expression.

Man! I hope these bitches didn't see me," holding his face with his hand.

Dex

Not one second later, "Whasup Dex?" spoke Flower in a deep toned voice, pretending to sound like a guy.

Dex never gave eye contact, but he wasn't fooled. He exhaled. "Hey..." dryly.

Flower chuckled. "Hey...? Damn, is that all the bitch gets that made your wildest fantasies come true? No flags, confetti, or horns? What the fuck? What did I do to you?" walking around, taking a seat in Dex's booth.

"You ain't did shit to me," responded Dex. "Me and my man just came to have a drink, look at the ladies and just chill."

Right then, the waitress arrived with the drinks. "That'll be $32." Dex gave the waitress $40 telling her to keep the change.

"Now that's one thing I can say about you Dex. You're not stingy with the money," admired Flower.

"I'm no fool with it either," he countered. "I know when I'm being played."

Flower smirked. "I know you had a little attitude. Dex, I only made a $1000 off of you. What are you whining about? You fucked ten different women that day including Sin and myself, and we gave you an one on one afterwards. Ask anyone, you got off cheap." She then broke into laughter. "I had both you and Sin hollering like some bitches."

You sure did, agreed Dex, thinking back to that day.

Flower continued. "After that Dex, you just disappeared. Ain't heard from you or nothing. So what brings you around here tonight?" downing Coke's shot of patron.

Dex could tell this conversation wasn't just casual. Flower was fishing, pretending to be cordial, but couldn't conceal how she really felt.

Dex cut straight to the chase. "Listen Flower, I don't want Sin if that's what you're thinking. I'm just here to have a drink."

"Well that's good to know because Sin's not available."

The attitude and tone of Flower's voice offended Dex. He decided to tease her a bit.

"Yeah, but I sure am gon' miss sucking on Sin's pretty black nipples, and kissing around her long sexy neck. Eeww, and that pussy, can't forget about that sopping wet pussy between them long legs. Mmph!" he emphasized looking to Flower. "I'm gon' miss that ass."

"Well, I got me a shot of the ass last night," returned Flower. "And I'm gon' hit it again tonight. Too bad you can't anymore, and you're gonna be paying for it the rest of your life."

Dex grimed Flower. "What the hell are you talkin' about?" he stood.

"Muthafucka', don't play dumb! You know what!" she fiercely pointed. "All them nuts you was bussin' in Sin. I knew your nasty ass wasn't pulling out. In fact, I'll let Sin tell you herself. Hey Sin!" Flower called to the next booth. This was the moment Dex had feared; this was situation he was trying to avoid. He knew sooner or later he was going to have to deal with this problem, he just wasn't ready to deal with it now. *Shit! Why did Coke bring me here?* shaking his head, looking towards the ceiling.

Sin walked over and sat next to Flower.

"Hi Dex," she softly spoke.

"Hey Sin," Dex waved, starring at her breast.

Flower looked to Sin. "Tell him!"

Sin dragged her eyes back over to Dex.

"Dex, I'm pregnant."

Dex

Dex played it cool. "That's nice, who's the father?"

"You are!" Flower blurted in. "So get them pockets ready, 'cause we gon' run 'em!"

Dex put up his hand. "Flower please, I'm talking to her. So Sin, what makes you think you could possibly be pregnant by me?"

"'Cause you raw fucked her with no condom! 'Cause you was bussin nuts in her with your nasty ass...! That's why!" Flower again intervened.

"Flower, you and Sin done fucked a gang of dudes around here. You're like some type of sex broker. If the price is right, you're sold. Shit, I just saw you two three-way kissing with ol' boy in the next booth. I'm quite sure y'all done fucked and sucked his dreams away many times. How come it can't be his baby?"

"Sounds like you're calling us some hoes, Dex."

"You didn't hear me say that. But I am calling you and Sin some scandalous bitches. How are y'all going to try to run that old school, 'I'm pregnant' bullshit game on me? Dex I'm pregnant," he mimicked Sin. "That shit didn't even sound convincing. I spent a stack and a half trickin' with you bitches, and now y'all wanna try to play me? Bitch please.., I'm not a sucker like yo' boy Freddy."

Sin's unconvincing statement drew more doubt than ever. Dex could see she was no more than a puppet in this show and Flower was pulling the strings.

Sin began to remove herself from the booth, when Flower grabbed her arm. "Hold on baby. Dex, you and I go a long way back as kids. You were sweet on me and I was fond of you. But, I really don't ever recall you being a tough guy. So don't sit here disrespecting me and my girl by calling us scandalous bitches and hoes. 'Cause it takes a trick to define a hoe, and you're one of the biggest tricks I know, trick!" Flower then slid Dex a piece of paper face down. "That's the number you need to pay, or Sin has this baby and you pay more later. Lets go."

Sin stood up eyeing Dex. Flower then escorted her away.

Scandalous bitches! Dex turned over the paper reading the numbers. "$7000! Shiiid... It'll be a cold day in hell before they see any money from me."

Before long, the liquor ran through Dex. He went to the bathroom.

Standing at the urinal, Coke stepped to the urinal beside him. "Looks like you and Flower were in a heated discussion."

"Naw, you don't say," sarcastically returned Dex. "I told you I didn't want to come here. But look at this," showing Coke the paper Flower gave to him.

"$7000? Wow! Flower must don't know you're broke."

"Obviously she don't," shaking himself off, zipping his pants. "Speaking of broke, I came up with a plan to get that money out of my mother's house. I'll run it down to you later."

"Cool," failing to tell Dex he'd already retrieved the money himself. Coke then threw his arm around Dex shoulder. "Dex, don't you worry yourself over this thing with Flower or Sin. It's already taken care of. What I do want you to do though, is grab you one of these freaks and have a good time on me. I'm paying for it."

Coke think he's slick, thought Dex. *He's testing me again; testing me to see if I'm so wrapped up in Ahbicdee that I won't dare to sex another woman. This is clearly a test that I couldn't possibly fail.*

Dex

"That sounds like a winner, Coke. I'm over due for a good nut anyway. Let me find me a bad bitch. Be right back."

Dex briefly browsed the room and there she was coming off the stage. Five-foot-six, thick, light skinned with freckles and red hair. Dex grabbed her hand as she was passing by. "Hey baby. What's up?"

"Gas and the rent," she replied.

"Well let's talk and see if we come up with something to subsidize on the gas and the rent."

Within seconds, a price for sex was negotiated. Dex and "Red," as he kept on calling her agreed on $220 for an hour of play. Dex told Red he didn't need that long but the price was cool. Red insisted the fee be paid upfront. "No problem." After the payment was made, Dex along with Coke was led down a narrow hallway, to the room where the dancers pulled tricks. Red paid the $20 room fee. When they entered:

Dex wasted no time, pulling out his dick, requesting some head
Red thought about it, looking at Dex, scooting onto the edge of the bed
She examined his dick, looking it over, mumbling, "I hope you ain't got nothin'"
"C'mon girl, don't start that shit, I'm clean, just get'ta suckin'"
She first kissed it, licked it, then went deep down on his shaft
Slob leaked down his dick, passed his balls, onto his ass
The head was tight, Red was a pro, Dex's nut was coming on too quick
"Stop it! Hold up! Wait a minute! Gotta put the brakes on this shit."

Nasty D!ck

"I wanna fuck, lay on your back, position that ass in front of me
I'ma mash it, tear it down, get all in that fat pussy"
He placed one hand around her throat, the other gripped her hip
Dex started long dickin' Red, nibbling, biting her bottom lip
He pulled her hair, slapped her face, told her she was his bitch
Red was loving it, wanted more, couldn't find the words to say, 'Quit.'
"Fuck me daddy! Beat this pussy! Take me! It's yours!"
That's when shit really got wild, Dex slammed her onto all fours
From the back, his nose met her ass, he was suckin' her clit
Suddenly she reached under and started stroking his dick
The faster Red stroked, the faster Dex sucked
"Eeww... Right there baby!" she moaned. "You gon' make me cum
You eatin' the shit out'ta my pussy!" Red's body started to flinch
Out came waterfall as if she just pissed
On the sheets, the floor, cum was all over the place
"She's a squirter," Dex smiled, with pussy juice dripping from his face
"I came so hard, I should've paid you, boy, what did you do to me?
I'm sweatin, my heart beatin' fast, and I feel so woozy"
"Coke, you wanna fuck? Get sucked? Get a little brain?"
"Naw... I'm cool Dex, handle your business, just do yo' thang."
"You straight? Fuck it! Goin' for mine, 'bout'a get this nut"
Dex licked his finger, spreaded her ass and stuck it in her butt

Dex

He then put Red in a position she never experienced before
She was bent over, back against the wall, face to the floor
Dex was in control, Dick deep up in her soul
Making her pussy wetter, working that brown booty hole
The quick, fast strokes suddenly came to a halt
Dex pulled out frowning, as if he had a mouth full of salt
He grabbed himself, jacked himself, became weak in the knees
The warm white shower skeeted towards Red's feet
She stuck out her tongue to sample the sweet babies
Love was all over her face, dripping like thick gravy
Red then tried to kiss Dex with love still on her lips
But Dex nudged her back, "Hold up baby. I ain't with that shit!"
He slipped on clothes, "C'mon Coke, lets ride"
"Oh, you just gon' fuck me and leave. Ok cool, that's fine"
"Listen girl, I served you, you served me, now I gotta go"
"Well, are you ever gon' call on me again?"
"Yeah I'ma call you. Call you a hoe"

As Dex and Coke made their way back out onto the floor, two police detectives in suits were headed in their direction. Dex turned white in the face. His hands turned to butter. He felt like he was about to shit on himself.

Coke peeped it. "Man the fuck up!" Stand your ground!" he whispered to Dex.

Just then, the two detectives walked passed the pair but not before winking at Coke.

Coke turned his head to the left indicating, "*Over there.*"

The detectives approached Flower and Sin seated at a booth with five other guys, drinking, smoking, laughing and talking loud. When the detectives pulled their badges, the five men dispersed with no question asked.

One of the detectives pulled out his cuffs. "Flower Roberts, would you please step out from the booth?"

Flower was shaken. "Am I under arrest? What is this about? This must be some type of mistake," standing from the booth, starting to cry.

"No ma'am, no mistake. You're under arrest for the murder of your husband, June Howard," clapping the cuffs around her wrists.

Sin was going hysterical trying to attack the officers. "Let her go! Let her go! She didn't do nothing!"

The other dancers and customers were starting to take notice.

"Get her. Calm her down," instructed Coke to Dex.

Dex rushed over restraining Sin. "Calm down. It's gon' be okay. It's gon' be alright."

The detective afterwards led Flower away.

Dex soon calmed Sin's nerves. "Let me get you a drink. I'll be right back," he told her.

Dex returned to the bar. "Damn, that scared the shit out of me Coke! I thought maybe Ahbicdee had gone to the police. But it turns out, they were here to arrest Flower for her husband's murder. Wonder how they found that out?"

"Me, I told them," said Coke.

"You? How? Why?"

"Beause that bitch Flower is a snake. I told you about her 20 years ago, but you didn't hear me. Turns out, Freddy is the one who came up with the plan for Flower to murder her husband. After she did it, she unknowingly confessed on his video camera how she carried out the plot. She and Freddy supposed to have split the money in the safe but being the greedy, money hungry, bitch that Flower is, she

Dex

played Freddy's dumb ass. He always threatened to send that video in to the police, but he didn't. He wouldn't. He still loved her ass. But I don't give a fuck about her. So, I obtained the disk and sent it in myself. Flower didn't know it, but she fucked with the wrong one. Told you Dex, I got your back."

Dex shook his head. "Coke, I'm glad you're on my side because you're one mean muthafucka'."

"Yeah I know. I tell myself that all the time."

Dex ordered Sin's drink, but he couldn't help to wonder why Sin wasn't arrested, since she was in on her own father's murder.

Sin's drink came. "Hold on," said Coke, pulling a small baggie of powder from his pocket. "This is Sin's drink, right?"

"Yeah, but..."

Coke emptied the white, powdery substance into the drink, and stirred it. "Make sure she drinks it all."

"What is that?" asked Dex, hoping it wasn't poison.

"It's Miferprex, an abortion pill sold overseas, illegal here in the states. This is for those who get away with murder, but don't confess it on tape, if that answers your question."

"I don't know about this Coke."

"Sin's pregnant by you whether you believe it or not, Dex. Do you want a child by a woman who assisted in the killing of her own father? What do you think she'll do to us?"

Dex's eye browse lifted.

Coke handed him the drink. "Make sure she drinks it all."

Dex walked over to the table apologizing for the delay. Sin didn't care. She didn't care about anything but

Nasty D!ck

Flower. She gulped the drink down in one shot. Dex got her two more drinks after that and Coke medicated her drinks two more times as well. Two days later, Sin would hemorrhage to death on the toilet from an overdose on abortion pills.

Dex

Candles flickering around a Bed

One month had passed. Since that time, Dex and Ahbicdee had seen one another almost every day. Nothing sexual had yet occurred, not even a kiss, but the magnetic connection was clearly there. The two talked about their goals and expectations out of life. They conversed about their past relationships, present, and how it would be if they'd gotten together. Feelings grew and the conversations between Dex and Ahbicdee started to become personal, very personal.

Sitting on the park bench, "Dex, the last 30 days with you have been fun, exciting and therapeutic for me," said Ahbicdee. "I just want to start off by saying thank you," squeezing Dex's hand. "Before you, I felt dead on the inside. I felt trapped. My life was repetitious. You know what I mean? I would go to work, come home, cook, and listen to my husband talk trash. We didn't go anywhere; we didn't do nothing; we didn't even talk about nothing; just absolutely no communication. It was the same thing, day in and day out. But with you Dex, it's different. You're a great listener. You have good conversation, you're great company, period. I mean, sometimes a woman just needs someone to talk to besides her girlfriends, who will just listen to her problems with no feedback or personal judgments about the situation.

And, I've found that in you Dex. It's been a very short time, but you make me want to love you," kissing Dex hand.

Dex melted like a Hershey's chocolate bar. Usually in a case like this when Dex knows he has a woman's mind open; has her mentally stimulated to where she couldn't see past any of his bullshit, he would seal the deal by going for the sex, which at this point was no challenge. After that, it would be her car keys, credit card and then her bank account. There was no love. But Dex didn't feel this way towards Ahbicdee. He could never use her up or dog her out. He wouldn't do anything to put her in harms way, regardless of what Coke said. Dex loved Ahbicdee that much.

Dex kissed Ahbicdee's hand in return. "I want you to meet my mother," he said starring into her eyes. "She told me I never brought a girl home that I thought I might be in love with, but I think I am now."

"Aww..."

Right then, Dex and Ahbicdee locked into their first kiss.

"But Dex, I'm married and besides, I thought you told me you and your mother had a big falling out."

"We did. I'm just hoping her meeting you will smooth it out."

"I doubt that Dex. I don't know if this is a good time."

"Please baby, for me?"

Ahbicdee grinned, loving the way Dex called her baby.

"Okay Dex, I'll meet your mother. But, can we just sit here and talk a little longer?"

"Anything for you baby," again kissing her lips.

Dex

Ahbicdee then went back in time telling Dex how her father one day just up and left when she was six years old. She told Dex of how sweet her father was towards she and her mother. How he cooked her breakfast, took her to the park, the movies and even braided her hair.

"He was such a sweet man Dex. And for him to disappear on me like that broke my heart," Ahbicdee sobbed.

Dex tried to put his arm around her back.

"No, no. I'm okay," wiping her tears. "Just let me finish. But, a young girl growin' up without a father is so hard. You tend to start searching for that father figure in other men who mean you no good. Dex, my heart is good as gold, but my vulnerability has taken me into some dark places. I can remember back when I was fourteen."

Ding, ling, ling, ling! chimed the door's bell as I entered the meat market. "Hello Mr. Hopkins," I greeted walking up to the counter.

"Well hello there Ahbicdee," Mr. Hopkins smiled. "It's only eleven o'clock. You're early. Wasn't expecting you for work until five."

I thought of a lie real quick. "Uh... today was the Mathematical part of the MEAP test, *(Michigan Educational Achievement Program)* so after most of the students finished testing, the school released us early for the day. Tomorrow is the English part of the test," I thickened my lie.

Mr. Hopkins shook his head. "You're a smart girl Ahbicdee. I'm proud of you. Come around this counter and give me a hug," taking off his apron.

I closed my eyes and tightly squeezed Mr. Hopkins. He felt warm, strong, and comforting just like daddy did years ago. He made me feel safe always referring to me as the daughter he never had. As I leaned against Mr. Hopkins chest, inhaling his cologne, I opened my eyes to see the other reason why I was there; Alfred, Mr. Hopkins oldest son who was starring at me through the stained, plastic divider, which separated the rooms. Alfred was fine as wine. This boy had it going on. All the girls liked him. They would come up to the meat market asking for him, being nice to me, talking to me about him thinking I was his little sister. I felt like I was part of the family.

So one day, this pretty girl came up to the market asking for Alfred. She didn't look happy at all, but I didn't think anything of it. Mr. Hopkins was gone. I was the only one up front running the store. Alfred was in back cutting meat. I called him several times, but I guess he couldn't hear me over the meat cutter. So, I went to the back to tell Alfred a young lady was at the counter asking for him. As I was headed back up front, I heard, "Get the fuck out my store and never come back, or I'ma kill your ass!" sounding like Mr. Hopkins voice. When I stepped through the divider, the girl was outside walking away. Mr. Hopkins was taking off his coat, smiling.

"Did any customers come in?" he asked.

I picked my face up like I didn't hear a thing.

"Five or six," I responded dismissing the unseen incident.

From there Dex, I should've known something wasn't right. That girl was no older than sixteen or seventeen and didn't deserve to be talked to like that by any man. But Mr. Hopkins was like a daddy to me and Alfred like my big brother. I loved them like I thought they loved me. So, going back to me and Mr. Hopkins hug. When we released from our hug, he kissed my forehead and ran his finger down the middle of my palm. I thought it was cute. Alfred squint his eyes and raised his brow.

Dex

"Hi Alfred," I spoke walking pass him in the back.

As I was putting on my apron, he asked, "What are you doing here? I thought I told you to never come back here anymore," squeezing my arm.

"Ow! That hurts Alfred. Why are you being so mean to me all of a sudden? I know you have a lot of girlfriends, but I really like to be around you," trying to hug him. But Alfred rejected me, pushing me away.

"Ahbicdee, I'm twenty years old. I'm not your big brother and my father is not your daddy. You've known us, what? A month? You don't have a clue. Please Ahbicdee, quit this job and don't come back."

I stood with my arms folded and tears in my eyes. It seemed Alfred was taking away the family I always wanted.

"Is everything alright back there?" hollered Mr. Hopkins.

"Yeah, fine pop! Ahbicdee will be up in a sec!" Alfred clicked on the meat cutter, and then put his finger to his lips. "Sshh..." He grabbed my hand and led me to a room hidden behind a false wall. I looked up and down, and all around. The room was painted black with mirrors on the ceiling. I can remember panties and bras being scattered throughout the room. And the last thing I could remember were candles flickering around a bed in the middle of the floor. I was scared to death Dex. I just wanted to get the hell out of that room and out of that market.

Suddenly, Mr. Hopkins appeared behind me. He gave Alfred a grim look, then myself.

"Well now Alfred, seems we have a willing participate who skipped school to be here today."

Just then, things went dark.

"So what happened?" asked Dex urgently.

Nasty D!ck

"Well, when I awoke, paramedics and police were on the scene. It seems Mr. Hopkins and Alfred had been raping and torturing under aged girls for years. Most were employees like myself who fell for Alfred's good looks and Mr. Hopkins warm fatherly like welcoming. They lured their victims by drugging them or most times cuffing their noses and mouths with a rag containing chloroform, knocking them out. After that, they'd have a good ol' disgusting time and snap naked photos."

"Aww! That's terrible," commented Dex. "How did the police know you were in that secret room?"

"The police already knew about the room. They had the place surveillanced and knew I had never came out of the building. They were gonna raid the market that morning, but I just happened to skip school that day, so the police reevaluated their raid plan for my safety."

"Wow! That's some shit."

"Yeah. In their raid, the police found blindfolds, handcuffs, mouth gags and a stack of pictures, which was the most incriminating evidence. The pretty girl who I mentioned came in the market asking for Alfred?"

"I remember."

"She was a victim of theirs two years ago. Police sent her in there wearing a wire hoping to get Alfred talking to strengthen their case, but Mr. Hopkins foiled that plan. It didn't matter though. Those nude pictures along with my testimony and the seventeen other girls they victimized, put Mr. Hopkins away for life."

"Damn... He deserved it anyway. What about his son, Alfy?"

"You mean, Alfred?"

"Yeah... him?"

Dex

"Dex, would you believe they let this fool out on bond. When his court date came of course he was a no show. Now, the police did end up catching up with him two months later. But that was because he was in the hospital requiring medical attention. Somebody cut Alfred up bad. The police suspect it was the parents of one of the victims. Alfred said it was a young kid about fifteen or sixteen he'd hit on a bike, but that report couldn't be confirmed."

All in, Dex's lip hung in question. "Just curious, what did this dude Alfred look like?"

"Mmm... He had sandy brown hair. A thin mustache with an albino coloration. Don't tell me you know him?"

"Naw, but it sounds like partner got what he deserved as well," thinking, *The world is a small place.*

"My daddy was in my life up until I was five years old," added Dex. "But we'll talk about him another time. Ahbicdee, can I ask you a personal question about what you just told me?"

Ahbicdee placed her hand over Dex's hand. "Ask me whatever you want. I'm that comfortable with you."

Dex stroked her hand in return, asking, "Did those men rape you?"

"Yes, they did," she boldly answered trying to stay strong. "I also believe this is the reason why I can't bare children. My husband and I have tried since we've been married, but I can't seem to get pregnant. Even my best friend Ché who couldn't find a man is having a baby."

Dex turned his head on that note.

Ahbicdee continued. "It just saddens me Dex to know I can't do the one thing a woman was set on this earth to do, and that's have children. Those bastards!" she again broke into tears. Dex sat on the bench consoling Ahbicdee for another hour.

Nasty D!ck

Out Done

"I really shouldn't be here. You heard what he told me the last time."

"Fuck him! This is my house. Now are you gon' just stand there naked looking stupid? Or are you gon' come get some of this juicy wet pussy?" Cree taunted, opening her legs, driving her fingers in and out of her pussy, tasting herself.

Duck was on brick. He was so hard, pre-cum leaked from his tip. He wanted Cree bad, but felt it would be disrespecting Dex.

"Cree, I... Uh..."

"I... Uh... my ass Duck," grabbing his hand, not wanting to hear that shit. "You gon' fuck me!"

Cree lined her lips up with Duck's, at the same time grabbing his dick steering it inside her ecstasy of love.

"Don't play with me. This is my shit," she outright told him.

Cree was so wet, they both could hear the pop sounds her pussy made from every stroke Duck took. Suddenly, he jumped up and cringed his fingers and toes, blowing air.

"What's the matter with you?" she asked, looking at him weird.

"I had to pull out or I was gon' cum. That shit feel too good," pacing the floor, trying to settle the nut he felt at the tip of his dick.

"Damn, you just got in it," complained Cree. She then turned over smiling knowing her pussy was the bomb. Duck was looking at Cree's ass, laid on her side.

Dex

Eeww... Dex was right. Cree's pussy get so wet, you can't even fuck it. Gotta pull out. Mmph... Look at that ass; so sexy. Okay Duck, calm down, calm down. You're too excited. 'Cause if you don't, you gon' bust fast. Think about... fuckin' your grandma.

Duck then took a couple of deep breaths.

"Okay baby, I'm ready," psyching himself up.

Cree turned onto her back.

"'Bout time, I was beginning to think you didn't want me," opening her legs.

Duck didn't respond too busy concentrating.

Fuckin' my grandma. Fuckin' my grandma, he repeated in his mind, climbing into the bed.

At this time Dex was pulling up outside. He needed to grab a few things before he and Ahbicdee's stay at the room tonight. He looked up at the house. It was daytime and a nice day. But the front door, which usually stood open, was closed and the blinds were pulled.

"This shit don't look right," suspicious.

"I can't hold it back! I'm gon' cum!" moaned Duck trying to fight the feeling. "Gotta pull out," trying to get up.

But Cree clamped her legs around his, locking him in. She then caressed his face.

"I want you to feel good baby. Let it go. I got you."

If Duck wanted to argue her decision, his time had already run out.

"Uh...! Uh...!" his body shook, gripping the sheets, icing her cake.

Cree was about to get hers as well concentrating, thrusting her hips, when she heard, Cling! Cling!

"Awe shit!" her eyes bucked.

Nasty D!ck

The sound of keys chiming in the front door sent her into action. "C'mon! C'mon!" she whispered in panic. "You gotta go! Dex is here!"

Duck quickly snapped out of his comatose like state, grabbing for his pants. He was shirtless, but out that side window in record time, only to find Dex standing behind him.

"You're slick cuz, but you ain't that slick," said Dex. Cree looking out the window sighed feeling ashamed.

Dex was on a rampage inside the house.

"So, you two muthafuckas' just gon' keep disrespectin' me, right? Fuckin', suckin' and doin' whatever it is y'all wanna do under the same roof my kid sleeps under, huh?" he stated pacing the floor, eyeing both Duck and Cree seated on the couch.

"But big cuz..."

"Shut up Duck! Shut the fuck up!" pointed Dex. "I'm so pissed at you right now, I could just beat yo' ass."

Duck held his head down towards his lap.

"And you bitch!" redirecting his finger at Cree. "You ain't shit! I told you before he's family, and you still fucking him!"

Dex continued degrading Cree bringing up her past; speaking bad about her sister, even a few words about her mother. Out of anger, Dex was mentally killing Cree until she had enough.

"Fuck you Dex!" she sprung from the couch. "You ain't shit either. Like you got your priorities all in order, muthafucka' you're broke. You don't have a job. You ain't nev'a had a place of your own; living with your mother for the last thirty-five years. And family, I know you're not talking? That twisted, fucked up, dysfunctional family you

Dex

have ain't half right in the head, including you. I wish you would hit me," seeing Dex ball his fist. Cree took a step back.

"See there, you can talk shit but can't handle shit. You've always been that way Dex. But since we're talking about the past, lets focus on what you've done. Now, my child was your first, and at this time you were my man. So how is it that you suppose to have been my man, but you went out and fathered three more children? Answer that for me since I'm the one who ain't shit."

Dex stood quiet.

Cree carried on. "Now at this time, the streets is talkin', but you're my man. So, I'd rather hear the story from your mouth. But when I confronted you about if or not you had children with other women, you lied to my face, telling me no. Regardless of how I would've felt Dex, I rather you had told me the truth. It kind'a made me lose a little respect for you behind that, 'cause what kind of man denies his own flesh and blood that he put here on this earth? Answer that for me, since I'm the only one standing here who's the bitch that ain't shit. But now, let me tell you how I found out about Dex's fourth child, that he again tried to deny," she said informing Duck. "My sister and I have different mothers, so we don't really look alike. Anyway, I take Gigolo Tony *(Dex)* here with me to a barbeque. Soon as we get there, he's ready to go. He's jittery, moving around, trying to hide his face. Just then, my sister's sister, who I hadn't seen in three years walks up to me and speak. We hug and then I go trying to introduce her to my man, and she says that's her child's father, talking 'bout Dex. Tore me down, do you hear me? Immediately, she and I fell out behind that shit, but after a while, we both realized, it wasn't our fault. It's him, Mr. Nasty Dick standing there."

Nasty D!ck

"Alright Cree, dammit! You've made your point. I have treated you like trash over the years. I'll admit that. I'm sorry."

"No Dex, an apology is not good enough for how I feel; the hurt won't erase away with just words. My heart bleeds because of how you've dogged me. You didn't take me anywhere. You didn't buy me nice things. Not a card, a flower, nothing to show your appreciation for me. I guess I just wasn't good enough for you," wiping her eyes. "And I've always taken good care of our son, whether you were able to contribute or not."

Dex felt like a heel. He knew everything Cree spoke was the truth. It wasn't that she was never good enough for him, it's just he ran around town trying to juggle his time between five and six other women who he now realized didn't matter, neglecting the one who really cared.

The situation for Duck was awkward. Here he was seated on his cousin's, ex-woman's couch, after being caught again for the second time sexing his cousin's, ex-woman, listening to his cousin and his ex-woman dispute over the past. Duck was in thought. *This is an incredible, weird, and fucked up situation I've gotten myself into. I really just want to get up and leave, but how do I do that? What would I say? Hey Cree, thanks for the best sex I ever had in my life, hope to do it again, see ya' later. Or, hey Dex, you fucked my momma, I fucked your ex-woman. Why be mad, just call it even, peace.* Duck tickled himself on the couch. He knew neither of those exit lines would fly, so he remained silent.

"But Cree, what in our past do you feel entitles you to mess around with my family member?" asked Dex, unable to understand.

"Everything Dex. Duck may be young, but he has charm and personality. He's fun, sensitive to my feelings,

Dex

and most of all, he's there. In some ways, you are these things now Dex, but not when I needed you. It's too late. I'm sorry. Lets just be parents to our son."

Dex usually was quick with his words, but what could he say after that? What come back line could he use? He came up with nothing. He thought about going Rambo on Duck and Cree's asses, but a jail sentence wasn't in his plans. Dex exhaled a breath.

"Let me get my things."

"Well Dex, I didn't ..."

"No Cree, you were right. I'm thirty-five and I never had my own place. It's time for me to grow up, move on and take some responsibility for myself. But thanks for letting me stay."

As Dex was gathering his belongings, Duck came up behind him. "Big cuz, I apologize man. I feel terrible. I didn't mean for this to happen."

Dex turned around. "Fuck it Duck. You were only doing what your old man and I taught you. Besides, don't nothing happen that wasn't already written. This was meant to be." He then continued to gather his apparel.

Dex loaded the last of his belongings into the car. He looked onto the porch to Cree. Her face seemed brighter, happier, like the cloud was gone from around her head.

Dex couldn't help but to wonder was he a burden to Cree? Did she feel obligated to take him in because he was the father of her child? Did she really like Duck or was this some type of act. Dex's questions were answered when he pulled off, looking into his rearview mirror. Both Duck and Cree rushed back inside the house, slamming the door. Dex, a little jealous and a little pissed off shook his head. *Damn, I was out done by a 19 year old kid. I guess Duck really did have game.*

Nasty D!ck

Where Do You Want It At?

"That's bullshit Coke!" ranted Freddy with his hand. "This was not the plan!"

Coke leaned his head against the steering wheel in frustration. "Dex ain't fuckin' Ahbicdee, Freddy. He assured me that, he's just working her in slow. The situation is handled, just be cool."

"Fuck cool! Shit is collapsing around me. My wife doesn't talk to me, she won't cook for me, and she won't fuck me no more. She might as well be dead. Then, I got Ché who's pregnant, who wants to be with me, who is also no longer fuckin' me. On top of that, Flower who I really didn't trust, who owes me money I know I will never see, is now lookin' at life in prison. What else could go wrong?"

Freddy again asked Coke for the third time. "A man, did you send that confession DVD of Flower in to the police? I'm just asking."

Coke gave Freddy a monstrous glare.

"Listen muthafucka', you're offending me. I told you no the last two times you asked me that question. I had no problems or issues with that bitch. Why and how would I send the DVD in? I don't know where you keep your personal video collection."

Freddy scratched his head. "What about Dex? Did he have any beef with Flower?"

"Nope, none that I knew of." Changing the subject, "Freddy, who else knows where you keep your DVD's? Answer that, and that's who sent it in to the police."

Both their eyes met. "Ahbicdee," in unison.

"See, there you go," said Coke. "It's always the wife."

Freddy punched his palm. "That bitch!"

Coke steered himself out of the way of suspicion indirectly blaming it on Ahbicdee. He then glanced at Freddy who appeared to be coming to tears. *I know he's not sobbing over that broad Flower,* taking a closer look. *Yeah, he's crying. Freddy's soft as a baby's ass.*

Coke wanted to scold Freddy, but took a different approach to the matter. "Freddy, I know you still love Flower. A child most times creates that bond between two people."

Freddy gave Coke a look of surprise.

"Yeah, I knew. I knew years ago you and Flower had a child who died at birth. But those chapters in your life are now closed, Freddy. It's time to move on man, move closer to someone who can give you what you want, and you and I both know what that is; another child. Ahbicdee couldn't do it. What good is she if she can't bare a child for her husband? Doesn't matter, her future isn't even up for discussion. I'm not telling you what to do Freddy, but if I were you, I would embrace the one that is trying to embrace me, and why not? She is carrying your seed."

Freddy wiped his eyes looking to Coke.

"That's right Freddy, I'm speaking of Ché. Go to that woman and express your feelings. Tell her what a joy it is for her to be carrying your child. It's a gift, a fresh start, a new family. Don't deny yourself life's gifts."

Freddy gave a steady nod of his head as if the word was being preached to him. Coke's words were strong and uplifting and made a lot of sense to Freddy.

Coke continued. "Here's what you do, go on over to Ché's place about 9:30, 10 o'clock tonight. Take with you some cheese, some grapes, crackers, maybe a sausage, a bottle of wine, and a candle. Set it all up, and then tell her how you feel. And I guarantee, you'll be swimming in that pregnant pussy before you know it. They say it's the best sex."

"It is!" cosigned Freddy already imagining himself in it. "Thanks Coke. I didn't know what to do before now. I'ma get home and start gathering what I need. I appreciate you man," exiting the passenger door.

Before closing the door, he looked to Coke. "To be honest Coke, I thought once upon a time you wanted to kill me. I thought you didn't like me. I guess it was just all in my head," smiling, closing the door.

Coke returned a smile, pulling away. *I don't.*

****

Dex

Dex pulled up in the parking lot of his mother's housing complex, spotting Ahbicdee seated in her car waiting on him. He exited his car walking up to hers.

"I see you found the place okay."

"Yeah, the directions you gave me where pretty simple. I've been out here for about ten minutes. I'm curious though. Is your mother moving? She has a lot of curb side garbage to be picked up."

Dex, at first not paying attention, looked. His bed, dresser, nightstands, lamps, clothes, pictures; anything having to do with him was thrown out. "What the fuck?"

Barbara had come home that day to see the disturbing sight of her front door off its hinges, lying on the floor. Most neighbors couldn't confirm, but said the perpetrator appeared to resemble Dex. They claimed to have stayed inside of their homes because of the weapon he toted in his hand.

Ms. Bryer *(the old lady)* affirmed the man she saw was Dex, but doubt surfaced around her statement because of her cataract eyesight. But there was no doubt in Barbara's mind. She knew who perpetrated the crime. She also knew it was only a matter of time before he returned.

Dex walked up to the curb.

"This is all my shit!" he told Ahbicdee, picking up a pair of his underwear from off the ground. He afterwards looked to his mother's new front door, ready to walk upon the porch.

Ahbicdee stopped him. "No Dex. Just let it be, for now," she encouraged, holding his hand.

"But..."

"Baby, trust me. You'll only make it worst."

The soothing voice and soft touch relaxed Dex's anger.

Nasty D!ck

Barbara watched Dex and Ahbicdee from the peephole in the front door, gather and load their cars with his belongings.

"Good riddance," feeling like a weight had been lifted from her shoulders.

Dex hated that his bedroom set had to remain behind. He stared at it with his hands behind his head.

"Don't worry about it, Dex. We'll get a new one when we get our own place," Ahbicdee smiled.

Dex tried to hold it back, but his smile came through. Ahbicdee made him feel good.

"Do you want these?" she asked, holding up two DVD's.

"Yeah, bring them."

She placed them inside her purse.

Finally, the cars were loaded to capacity. It was time to go. Before leaving, Dex grabbed Ahbicdee's hand leading her onto his mother's porch.

"I know you can see me ma!" he spoke to the red door. "You've always been a peephole watcher. I just wanna say that I'm sorry for how our relationship turned out. We've always been so close and able to talk about whatever. Hopefully, in time you and I can become friends again and share a few laughs. I'm also here to say, this is the new love of my life. Her name is Ahbicdee."

Barbara scanned Ahbicdee up and down far as the peephole would allow her to see. *She's beautiful,* thought Barbara.

Dex continued. "She's sweet, she's kind, and she's beautiful ma. She has a heart of gold. I just wanted to finally bring you home a girl to meet that I'm in love with. And... I guess that's it."

Dex

Dex kissed his hand and put it to the door. "Love you ma."

Barbara silently watched in tears as Dex and Ahbicdee walked away.

Just as Dex and Ahbicdee were getting into their cars, Dex waved. "Hi Ms. Bryer, long time no see. How are you today?" he asked as she stepped out of her front door.

Ms. Bryer put up her middle finger, as to say, *Fuck you.* Dex was surprised.

Ahbicdee laughed. "Gosh Dex, what did you do to her. That old lady has a beef with you."

Dex hunched his shoulders really not concerned. The couple then rode off, headed to the motel.

At the room, Dex sat at the edge of the bed appearing to be distraught. It bothered him that the relationship between he and his mother had deteriorated. It seemed to him he was losing the key women who had been a big part of his life, now thinking of Cree.

My life, my life, he thought holding his face. *Could it get any worse?*

Right then, a pair of warms hands embraced around Dex's neck, and then slowly worked themselves across his shoulders. The deep tissue, thumb and knuckle massaging down his back had him purring like a kitten. Suddenly, he felt a hot mouth clamp down onto his neck. A tongue licking around his ears soon followed. Dex's toes curled with anticipation not knowing what was next.

Ahbicdee was in control, taking charge. She kissed his forehead, his right eye, the left eye and then his nose; down to his chin, both sides of his neck, afterwards back up to his lips. Tongues began exploring one another mouths. Lips were being sucked, pulled and stretched like taffy.

Nasty D!ck

Dex's nature was on the rise. Butterflies were in his stomach. Touching, holding and squeezing Ahbicdee's body was breath taking. From the way Dex was feeling, it was if sexual for-play had taken on a whole new meaning. But Dex began to feel weird, feel as if maybe he was rushing Ahbicdee, as if he were taking advantage of her.

"Baby, baby, baby!" Dex said, halting Ahbicdee from her seductive attack.

"What!" Ahbicdee frowned. "Is something wrong?"

Dex looked into her eyes. His heart skipped a beat.

"No baby. There's nothing wrong. I just didn't expect..."

"Expect what, for me to be so aggressive?"

Dex nodded with a curious expression.

Ahbicdee again kissed his lips.

"Thank you baby for considering my feelings. I have been through a lot lately. But like I told you, spending time with you has helped me tremendously. I'm stress free now. I can see better, think clearer. It's like a resurrection of me; a metamorphosis from my old self. From now on Dex, I'm doing what makes me happy. Do for myself, cater to me and quit trying to please and satisfy the needs of others, like my husband. Do you know the last time we had sex, three months ago, he fell asleep on top of me?"

Damn... thought Dex, speechless.

"Claiming he was tired. The time before that, he got up off me to watch a TV show, saying he didn't want to miss it."

Dex wanted to laugh, but held it back, shaking his head.

"So, if I'm coming off a little aggressive Dex, now you know why. It doesn't make me less of a lady in your eyes, does it?"

Dex

"Oh, No! No! No! Not at all," quickly defended Dex.

"Good. Then I won't have to excuse myself by telling you, I don't need your respect right now. I do need for you to quit acting brand new with me, peel these clothes off me, and come fuck the shit out of me. I need it," she added.

Dex was floored, not expecting to hear such language coming from an angel. But, it turned him on even more. His thoughts started running wild, wondering how far would Ahbicdee go? How freaky could Ahbicdee get? To test the waters, Dex took off his own clothes. Standing naked, he put his right foot onto the edge of the bed, the left remained planted on the floor. "Come make love to daddy's dick," he requested, hoping he hadn't went too far.

Ahbicdee's eyes rolled, her neck snapped and mouth opened like, *No he didn't.*

Dex could tell Ahbicdee was offended from the expression on her face. *Awe, I done fucked up,* his mind dreaded as she approached. Dex was preparing to apologize for his statement, that's until Ahbicdee dropped down onto her knees and positioned her mouth under his nuts.

Ahbicdee wanted to give Dex a piece of her mind. She wanted to frown up and tell him how she didn't suck dick, but that would be telling a lie. It would only be a front. It wouldn't be real to how she felt or to what she really wanted to do.

"I haven't done this in a long time," she told Dex, kissing and licking the insides of his thighs. "But I wanna do it for you."

Dex tilted his head backward feeling the heat of her mouth near his nut sacks. The arousing tease caused him to cringe and shake.

"Mmm... you like that baby?" now sucking his balls.

Nasty D!ck

Oh, Dex was liking it. Shit, he was loving it. It was so sexy to him how his brick hard dick was now laying across her nose and forehead.

But it would look sexier if my dick was in her mouth. Dex palmed the back of Ahbicdee's head with his left hand, twirling his dick around her lips with his right. He then thrust his hips forward riding the wave of her tongue. On contact, he sucked in the saliva from around his teeth. The head job was feeling like pussy. Ahbicdee then pulled his dick from her mouth.

"Come on now. All the way in, don't be shy."

With no shame, Dex slowly pushed far as he could past her tonsils, inching his way down her throat.

I love you bitch! he wanted to say, again sucking the saliva from around his teeth. If he didn't pull out now, that bomb was going to detonate in her throat.

"Awe... Why did you pull out baby? I was about to cum," whined Ahbicdee.

"Suckin' my dick was about to make you cum?" asked Dex.

"Yes. My panties are drenched."

"Well get them clothes off. Come bust that nut on this hard dick right here."

In two steps, Ahbicdee was naked. Dex looked her over; that chocolate brown skin, that long black hair, them petite, perky titties and that handful of ass. Ahbicdee didn't have the biggest ass, but it was a nice size ass. Something Dex could sink his teeth into.

She gave Dex the, *Come fuck me eyes,* asking, "How do you want it?" bending over the bed.

"Just like that, don't move," said Dex as he entered that creamy slit from the back, hitting bottom.

"Owe..." Ahbicdee jumped. "Be gentle baby, okay?"

Dex

Gentle? Fuck that. The role of control had reversed. Ahbicdee began taking erratic breaths, breathing like she was in labor. She felt as if the dick was pushing towards her heart. Several times she placed her hand between her ass and Dex's abdomen to lessen the blows, only for her hand to be slapped.

"Get it out the way, I said!" again slapping her hand, pushing harder inside.

Just then, Ahbicdee felt her asshole stretch wide open. The two fingers inside her ass felt like an enormous dick. She screamed several times into the pillow, ready to rip out the down feathers with her teeth. After a minute, the fingers inside her ass started feeling good. Her pussy became wetter and juicier. Cum suddenly bust loose from her body like out the neck of a water hose. Dex balls were soaked. He could feel the slickness of her pussy. He began pulling himself out until seeing the head, only to push deep back inside. *Long dickin' that ass.*

Ahbicdee was now wide open. She felt like there was nothing she couldn't handle. She was ready to fuck.

"Turn me over baby. Give it to me from the front." Ahbicdee laid on her back, holding her legs wide open. "Now gimme that dick. Beat this pussy up. Come fuck me, Dex," sliding her fingers in and out her pussy lips.

Damn... thought Dex. *This girl is a nympho.*

But without hesitation, he rammed his meat back inside her package, lifting her body with hard thrusts.

"Uh...! Uh...!" Ahbicdee screamed. "I didn't... I didn't think there was another man out there who could fuck me like you can. Weph! Why did I get married?"

Dex again worked his fingers back up inside her ass, at the same time, running his tongue over each of her breast. He pulled those long, black, raisin like nipples with his lips, one after the other; pulling, nibbling, biting, sucking, and with that hard dick, smashing up against Ahbicdee's clit, she began to go crazy.

"Oh! Oh! Oh shit! I'm cumin again! Oh fuck! I'm cumin. Dex!"

Ahbicdee began convulsing. She wildly kicked her legs. The multiple orgasms had her acting a damn fool. It didn't help her none either that Dex kept on fucking her. Ahbicdee couldn't take anymore.

"Dex baby... Please... baby. Cum for me, please... baby. I can't take any more."

Dex was in rhythm, stroking, fucking in a hard sweat. He loved that Ahbicdee was begging him to cum.

"You want me to bust baby?"

"Yes..."

"You want me to cum girl?"

"Yes..."

"Where do you want it? Where do you want me to bust it at? On your face, neck, chest? In you? On you? Where?"

"Wherever baby. Don't matter, just cum."

After ten more pumps, Dex started frowning. The orgasm within him displayed its ugly face.

"Uh...! Uh...!" loudly he groaned, trying to fuck through his nut, but it was useless. The orgasmic high was overwhelming, paralyzing any functions. "Uh...! Shit!"

Ahbicdee rubbed his back, welcoming his D.N.A. "It's okay baby."

"Damn... Damn, that was good. Shit, I don't even smoke and I need a cigarette. Whew!" catching his breath.

Ahbicdee laughed.

Dex

Dex gave her a puzzled look. "And you say your husband went to sleep up in that? Shiiid, that pussy's good. He's fuckin' somebody else. That's all that is."

Ahbicdee changed the subject not wanting to ruin the moment discussing her husband. "Dex, when I went home to get some clothes, I got this letter out the mailbox," pulling it from her overnight bag.

Dex read over the sender's name and address. *Claude Rayford? 323 Naamens St. Chicago, Illinois, 60616.*

He glanced at Ahbicdee in question.

"That's my father!" she explained in excitement. "After all these years, he found me Dex. He wants me to come visit him. Isn't that wonderful? Everything in my life is making a 180-degree turn for the better. I'ma have a new niece or nephew soon. I got a new man in my life. And I'm going to be reunited with my father. I'm so happy Dex," kissing his hand.

Dex gave a dry smile. He too found a letter with his property outside of his mother's house, but yet didn't want to reveal his own news. This was Ahbicdee's moment.

"So when do you leave to go see your father?" he asked.

"Believe it or not, I leave tomorrow. I'm so excited. Dex, I knew meeting you had to be heaven sent. I love you."

Dex just smiled, giving her a hug. He then checked the time. *8:30.* "Awe damn... I gotta make a run sweetie."

Ahbicdee's face twisted. "Right now?"

"It's not going to take long, I promise."

She had her doubts. "Alright then, well, they do have a DVD player in here. Is it okay if I watch one of those DVD movies I picked up outside your mother's house?"

"Sure, do whatever you feel."

Nasty D!ck

Dex afterwards threw on his clothes and was out the door.

.

Dex

Please... Don't Go

"So, do you really want this baby?" Ché asked Freddy.

He kissed and rubbed her stomach. "Yes, I really do want this baby," he replied sincerely.

Ché was overjoyed. She picked up her book of names off her nightstand, and laid on Freddy's lap.

"Now if it's a girl, here are some cute names Ahbicdee and I picked..."

Freddy jumped from the bed cutting her off. "Dammit Ché! What the fuck!"

Ché was startled. "What? What did I say?"

"Me and Ahbicdee this! Me and Ahbicdee that! Ché, you and Ahbicdee are not friends. You're fucking her husband. You are pregnant by her husband. You are involved in a conspiracy along with her husband to have her murdered. You two are no longer friends. What part of this do you not understand?"

Ché sat looking dumb, searching for an answer. "So, you don't want to see the names in the book she and I picked out?"

Nasty D!ck

Freddy held his face, shaking his head. *I can't believe this is the woman who's having my child.* "Ché, sometimes I think you hung around Ahbicdee just to shield your own insecurities; just to make yourself feel better. I'm going to take a shower." Freddy left out of the room, stopping at the linen closet. He grabbed a washcloth, a towel and then retired to the bathroom.

Ché lying across the bed was in thought. *You're so right Freddy, my unborn child's father. I have always been cute, had a body, and have been chased by many men. But for some weird reason, I couldn't keep one around. Why? I so many times cried in the mirror asking myself. Why won't any man stick around to get to know me? Was my beauty and body a curse? But you Freddy, I saw you five years ago watching me, wanting me, lusting over what every other man wanted, my body. But I knew Ahbicdee couldn't have kids. And I knew once you were inside these hips, you were gonna slip up. So call it what you wanna; insecure, unsure, uncertain, but bottom line is Freddy, I'm having your baby, boo.*

Just then, Ché turned her head looking to the hallway, thinking she saw something out the corner of her eye. She looked left, right, high and low. Nothing; she dismissed it, continuing to read her book of names. Suddenly, she saw it again.

"Freddy?" she called, again looking to the hallway. "Is that you? Quit playin' now. You know my ass is scary." Ché got out of the bed and slowly crept towards the door. "Freddy, please answer me," looking out into the dark hallway.

The only thing Ché could see was the light from the bathroom shining from up under the door. She could also hear the shower water beating against the wall. But from her bedroom door, to the bathroom, down that long, dark hallway, appeared to be a passageway into hells gate.

"Freddy...!" for the third time she hollered, again receiving no response.

Okay Ché, pull yourself together girl. This is your house. You walk this hallway fifty-eleven times a day.

Ché took her first step out the bedroom planting her back sideways against the wall. She repeatedly watched her back, her front, and her back again, taking baby steps, sliding along the wall. Ché was letting nothing or no one run up on her unexpectedly. Finally, she reached the bathroom door.

Bam! Bam! Bam! "Freddy! Freddy! Are you in there?" Are you okay?" looking on both sides of herself. Bam! Bam! "Freddy!"

Just then, the bathroom door opened. A thick cloud of steam rushed out. Ché stood back in fear unable to see. Suddenly, she screamed as Freddy appeared out of the mist. His hair and face covered with soap and shampoo, gave him a ghost like appearance. Ché slapped his arm.

"You scared me," feeling relieved.

"And you're getting on my fuckin' nerves, callin' my name and beatin' on the damn door like you're crazy."

"Freddy, I'm scared."

"Scared? Scared of what? This is your house."

"I know... But I thought I saw something."

"Ché, you're trippin'. Look, I'm dripping soap and water all over the floor. Let me rinse off and I'll be in there."

"Okay, but leave the bathroom door open."

Freddy walked back inside the bathroom.

Ol' scary ass girl.

Ché walked back towards her bedroom turning on every light she passed. When she entered her room, the door was slammed shut behind her.

Nasty D!ck

Freddy stood in the shower with his eyes closed, letting the hot water run over his body. It then dawned on him what Ché had said. *I thought I saw something.* Freddy's eyes opened. "Ché...!"

He stepped into the hallway naked and dripping wet. He looked up the hall to see the bedroom door was closed. A great fear plagued his body. His jog up the hallway turned into a desperate sprint. He burst through the bedroom door. What Freddy saw almost brought him to his knees. Ché was laying face down on the bed. Her hands and feet were duck taped behind her back. A plastic bag was wrapped around her head, also fastened with the duck tape. Freddy in a zombie like state rushed over to the bed, turning Ché over. Her open dead eyes stared back at him. Still, he tore the plastic bag from around her face, hoping for some sign of life, but there was none. Ché was gone. Freddy broke down into tears.

"Oh... Ché... Please... No! No! No!" squeezing her tightly. "Please baby... Don't go... Please... Oh... Lord. He then released her lifeless body, looking around the room, more than sure of who committed this crime.

Freddy then reached inside the nightstand drawer, pulling out his 45 automatic.

"C'mon out muthafucka!" pointing the gun at the closet; the only evident hiding spot anyone else in the room could be. He cocked his weapon. "You got until the count of three. "Two!" he started off.

The closet door opened. A knife first appeared from behind the door. Freddy swallowed continuing with a sharp shooters aim. Suddenly, a familiar face emerged from behind the door.

"Drop the knife, Coke!" yelled Freddy. "Drop the knife, or I'll drop you!"

Dex

"Drop me then," calmly said Coke.

Freddy's finger tightened around the trigger.

Coke read it in Freddy's eyes how anxious he was to kill him. Coke thought fast.

"Don't you at least want to know why I did it, Freddy, why I killed Ché? I know that big question mark of why is swirling around your head."

A single tear ran from Freddy's red eyes.

"I don't need for you to define to me why you killed my family. I already know why, 'cause your a sick fuck who needs to be put down, you multiple personality, schizophrenic, physco, sicko, son-of-a-bitch!"

Coke pointed with the knife.

"No! No! Freddy! We swore on our lives to never mention that!"

"We were kids then you fuckin' menace! How could I have let this go on for so long?" Freddy questioned himself. "I just stood by and let you destroy countless lives. Coke, It's time you left. Dex! Dex!" he called. Come on out of there! Don't let Coke suppress you any longer. Fight!"

Coke began to shake and tremble as Dex fought to come forth. "Freddy? What are you doing? Where? Where am I?" scanning the bedroom.

It appeared Dex and Coke were one of the same body; two different personalities under one host.

Dex mouth dropped open when he saw Ché tied up lying on the bed. "Is that? Is she? You killed her?" now defensive, discovering the knife in his hand, holding it in an upright position.

"Whoa! Calm down Dex. It is you Dex, right?" questioned Freddy.

"Yeah, it's me. Who else would it be?"

Nasty D!ck

Freddy kept his distance between them, but began to explain to Dex of another personality *(Coke)* within himself. He told Dex signs of his sickness began to surface when they were five years old, around the time when his father first left home. Freddy brought it to Dex attention how he waited on the porch everyday for six months for his father to return home from work.

"But he never did. After a while, Dex, you disassociated yourself from all of your friends, including me. Your mother couldn't figure out what was wrong with you. You just sat, and sat, and sat, staring from that upstairs bedroom window to the outside. Then one day, we heard you laughing and playing and it seemed like the old Dex we knew. Of course you talked to yourself a bit. The other kids and myself found it to be a little strange, but we all once upon a time had an imaginary friend. It wasn't until our teenaged years that we figured something wasn't right about you. Your mother's abusive boyfriend at the time was again beatin' on her and you went insane. You beat that man with that bat within two inches of his life in front of everybody. When you were acknowledged by friends and neighbors for protecting your mother, your response was, "I didn't do it for that bitch! I did if for Dex." Things to me then started to make sense. For some strange reason, I wanted to get to know this other side of you. To me, he was like no one else I'd ever met before. People talked about whooping ass and crackin' heads, but this other side of you was doing it; a for real bad ass. The more I hung around you, the more I understood him. It was like a light switch. He basically controlled your every move at will. That was until Ms. Barbara took you in to the doctor one day for an evaluation. You were diagnosed with schizophrenia. The medication the doctor prescribed you had you back to regular, boring old

Dex

Dex. The fucked up thing is, I didn't want you back. I wanted the other guy you had become. So, when I came to visit you one day, I switched your prescribed medication for some copycat vitamins. In no time, you were back to your new self. From there, Coke and I became friends. You were somewhat of a has-been in a social sense. I know, I must have been insane myself to befriend a sociopath. But everyday with him was new, exciting and unexpected. And nobody fucked with us. Then Flower came into the picture. She liked you, she was in to you. Coke didn't like that. He afterwards kept telling me how you were saying I couldn't get a girl, how you knew I was jealous of you and Flower's new relationship. I had already had Flower before. I really didn't want her. But the more Coke poisoned my ears with his rumors, the more I desired her. That's when he threw a cross between us. He planned it that way, the muthafucka'."

This was too much, but Dex knew it to be true. He continued to listen.

"And Dex, brace yourself for what I am about to tell you next. There's a third personality that I know you're not aware of; so sinister, so mean and evil that I can't believe I let myself become involved. You're also a child smuggler named, Ocknock Iyabo.

Dex knew of Coke, but never heard of this Ocknock. It was disturbing news.

"I... I... I don't know what to say Freddy. I guess I need help."

Freddy shook his head. "Dex, there is no helping what you have. It's only one way to cure it."

Dex took a hard swallow. He was blinking and stuttering. "There got... It must..."

"Sorry Dex, there's no other way," taking aim.

Nasty D!ck

Dex wanted to fall to his knees and beg Freddy for mercy. He wanted to drop down to the floor and scream, "Lord no! Please... don't kill me!" But he couldn't. Schizophrenic or not, he was still a man. "What about Ahbicdee?" Dex asked bargaining for time.

"What about her?"

"Remember, I'm supposed to kill her or she's going to the police."

"I'm not worried about Ahbicdee going to the police no more than Coke is. Now, who I was worried about going to the police is her," he pointed with the gun. "My baby laying over there dead on the bed."

"Who Ché?"

"Yeah Ché. She recorded Ahbicdee's conversation telling her about me kidnapping the little girl. She was gonna use that video to blackmail me, but she ended up pregnant by me and fell in love. I suspected Coke wanted to kill her, but I had no idea he followed me over here tonight. Talkin' bout cheese and crackers. It was all bullshit just for him to get close to her."

"Bravo muthafuckin' Sherlock Holmes!" said Coke, taking over the host.

"So, are you gon' shoot, or are you gon' stand there reading me my life story?"

Freddy frowned. "Muthafucka' What! Who you...?" Click! Click! Click! frantically looking at his gun, clueless to why it wasn't firing.

Just then, Coke swung his knife. Freddy stumbled two steps backwards, grabbing his throat. Blood filled his hands. He gasped for air falling onto the one knee, grabbing for Coke's leg. Coke stood aside with his knife in hand, smirking.

Dex

"Who says you cant bring a knife to a gun fight? I know you didn't know it Freddy, but I shaved the firing pin in your gun after I entered Barbara's house. Never let another man handle your weapon."

Freddy gurgled one final time before crashing face first to the floor. Coke set the house on fire and then went on his way.

****

Dex walked back into the motel room. Instead of a smiling face, he walked in to see Ahbicdee in tears. Closing the door, turning on the lights, "What's wrong baby?" rubbing her shoulders.

Ahbicdee pulled away from Dex, hopping up from the bed. She then turned towards him. "How could you do this to me, Dex? How could you be so mean and evil?" she cried. "I thought just maybe you were the one, someone different. But you're not. You're no different at all."

Dex's face wrinkled up. His heart began to ache. "I am different baby. I'm sorry," not knowing what he was apologizing for. *She knows. Ahbicdee knows about Freddy and Ché!* he panicked.

"Calm the fuck down," Coke voiced in Dex's mind. "She doesn't know shit. If she did, trust me, she would've already have run out that door. Nicely, ask Ahbicdee what is she talking about."

"Ahbicdee, what are you talking about baby?" asked Dex appearing to be back in control.

Ahbicdee grabbed the remote giving Dex a look that could kill. She then turned on the TV along with the DVD player. On the screen, Freddy was fucking Ché doggy style telling her how he couldn't get enough.

183

Nasty D!ck

Oh shit! Dex's eyes widened. How in the hell...? Ahbicdee pointed to their faces. "This is my husband fucking my best friend Ché! This is one of the DVD's I put in my purse earlier at your mother's house. You know my husband don't you? Where did you get this video from? Don't lie to me Dex!"

"I don't even know Freddy," Dex blurted.

Ahbicdee squint her eye. "How did you know his name? I've never told you my husband's name."

"Oh... Ew... Fuck me Freddy," came the sound from the television set.

"Does that answer your question? Ahbicdee I'm not..."

"No!" she said unsatisfied. "Where'd you get this video from?"

Dex had no dancing room. "From the video man, who sells DVD's. I bought it for $5. Could've got three for 10," he fabricated.

Ahbicdee sat on the bed crying. "I'm sorry Dex. I'm just so mad right now. I can't believe this. I expected some shit like this from Freddy, but not from Ché. She's my best friend, really my only friend."

Dex sat down next to Ahbicdee. He threw his arm around her back, leaning her face against his chest. "Baby, sometimes those people who we have been knowing forever are the ones who fucks us over. And those people who we meet later in life are the ones who holds us close," squeezing her arm.

"Thanks Dex," she smiled. "But I'm still mad."

Dex stood up. "No need to be mad. Freddy and Ché didn't understand how much of a beautiful person you are. You do still plan on going to visit your father in Chicago, right?"

Dex

"Of course."

"Well, c'mon Ahbicdee. Let's fly out to Chicago right now. Be adventurous, lets go."

Ahbicdee was excited. "Sounds good, but I don't have clothes here for the trip."

"It's Chicago baby. We'll shop when we get there."

Coke butted in. "Yeah Dex, that sounds real good. "But how can a broke muthafucka' buy plane tickets and shop in Chicago with no money?"

"With your money," Dex answered. "That's payback for that sex video of Freddy and Ché you forgot to mention to me."

Realizing his mistake, Coke said no more. Dex and Ahbicdee afterwards took off for Metro Airport.

Nasty D!ck

Ms. Smart Bitch!

The next day, Dex treated Ahbicdee to several of Chicago's high-end retail stores on The Magnificent Mile. They made a few purchases at the Gucci shop, afterwards the two hopped on over to the Chanel Boutique, where Ahbicdee found herself a camel colored handbag with gold lettering. Dex cashed himself out a pair of elephant tusk frame Cartier glasses; he and his newly announced sweetie then browsed through Victoria Secret. Last and final, the couple indulged themselves with a delicacy of treats at the Cheese Cake Factory.

Now back in their hotel room at the Marriott Suites, Dex indulged himself on the delicacy treat between Ahbicdee legs, french kissing her pussy. His tongue was on a sexual exploration driving in, out, and around her slit. Suddenly, he got freaky and experimental smearing cheese cake against her clit, eating it off. He then dropped the whole cake onto her pie. The tongue was in over drive dropping cowlicks on that ass; lickin', nibblin', suckin', soppin'. Ahbicdee was twitchin'; her mind was in a traumatic state of ecstasy. A tingling high rushed through her arms and legs, creeping towards her heart.

Dex

Oh God, she thought taking a hard swallow. What is this man doing to me?

Just then, Dex had Ahbicdee crouch over his face as if she had to piss. There, his lips and her clit again conspired into another wrestling match. She cupped her mouth to drown out her loud screams. Her juices dripped from her body into his mouth. Her legs began twitching with weakness from the lose of fluids. She suddenly lost her balance as her ass and pussy smashed into Dex's face.

"Oops, I'm sorry," she said embarrassed, hopping up. As Ahbicdee got up onto all fours, she once again found her body under attack. From behind, Dex's tongue launched a full squadron attack on that clit. His nose was planted in her ass. The oral sex was mind blowing, at the same time mesmerizing because of the mental connection. Ahbicdee's first and second nut was already built, on standby, waiting for Dex's tongue to hit that spot. Suddenly, her eyes bucked wide open, feeling his hot tongue swimming around her asshole. It felt good than a muthafucka', but Ahbicdee was in question. *Dex eating my ass out? It feels great, but all that kissing we've been doing is gon' stop, nasty!*

Before her thoughts were complete, or she had a chance to brace herself, Dex's tongue hit that spot giving her nut permission to fly. Her orgasm flowed forever and a day. She fell onto the bed like a dead body thrown into a grave. She could only lay and wait for the recovery process. Soon after, Dex with cheesecake and pussy juice still glistening on his face, stuck his tongue down Ahbicdee's throat. She gladly welcomed it in, licking his teeth and face clean with her tongue.

"Whew wee...!" Ahbicdee grinned. "Dex, you're a freak. You ate my pussy so... good. Are you ready to get yours?" running her hand across his dick.

Nasty D!ck

"You gettin' yours, is me gettin' mine," replied Dex.

"But you're so hard," jacking him with her hand.

"It's cool. It'll go down. We'll save mine for later."

Thank God, thought Ahbicdee. *Because I ain't got an orgasm left in me.*

She kissed Dex on the cheek. "Okay baby. It's one o'clock. I gotta start getting ready to go see my father. Are you sure you don't want to come with me to meet him? He'd love to meet you."

"I'm sure he would, but no sweetie pie, you go on ahead and get acquainted with your dad. I'ma stay here, lay back and take me some time to think."

"Okay." Ahbicdee again kissed his cheek. Dex then watched her cute booty as she pranced into the bathroom. He deeply inhaled loving his new woman. He heard the shower water being turned on, but he also could hear what sounded like Ahbicdee having a conversation. He hurried over to the bathroom door placing his ear against it, catching the tail end of her talking.

"And I know about you and Ché Freddy! You can have that bitch! I got me somebody new myself. So toodles asshole, and have a nice life!" Clap! the cell phone closed.

Dex afterwards crept back over to the bed, thinking, *I doubt if she was actually talking to Freddy.*

Twenty minutes later, Ahbicdee emerged from the bathroom fresh and clean. The sensuous aroma of Bath and Body works products lingered around Dex nose.

"Damn, you smell good," eyeing her towel wrapped body.

"Thanks baby. It's all for you."

"That's good to know. But is everything alright? I heard some yelling coming from the bathroom," fishing.

Dex

"Oh, I'm sorry. I called home leaving a message. I got a little heated with my words. My apologies to you."

"No, I understand."

Ahbicdee turned towards the vanity mirror ready to put her makeup on, when she sat crying, starring at herself.

"What's wrong?" asked Dex getting up from the bed.

"Freddy was right. I am damaged goods. I can't make no one else happy because I'm not happy with myself."

"Ahbicdee, that's not true. I've never been so happy with any other woman besides you."

Ahbicdee's teary swelled eyes looked up to Dex's face. "Really?"

"Yes. You're gorgeous, fun to be around, and beautiful at heart. You're blessed in so many ways. Now c'mon and get ready. You're gonna be late."

She tightly hugged Dex around his waistline and kissed his lips. "You make me feel so special. Visit my father with me, please?"

"Ahbicdee..." Dex rolled his eyes towards the ceiling. "I can't. You're married. How would that look? What would you tell your father?"

"I'll tell him that you're my new man. He doesn't know anything about me. So, will you come with me, please...? I can't do this alone."

This was going against everything Dex said he wasn't going to do. He knew this was a very bad idea. But after looking off into Ahbicdee's pretty brown eyes, and listening to her pleads, he couldn't deny her.

"Okay, I'll go," he found himself saying. Ahbicdee was ecstatic.

Coke laughed. "Oh boy, this outta be interesting. We're going to daddy's house."

Nasty D!ck

After getting dressed, they headed out to Ahbicdee's fathers house.

"309, 313, 319," Dex read the addresses.

Ahbicdee pointed. "That's gotta be the house up there where all those cars are."

They pulled up, creeping past 323 Naamens, taking an available parking spot five houses down.

"Wow!" said Dex looking into the rearview mirror. "I thought it was going to be a one on one reunion with you and your pops. This looks like a party to me."

"It sure does," agreed Ahbicdee, turned around looking out the back window. "Well, we might as well join it. Are you ready?"

Dex was hesitant unsure if this was the right thing to do.

Ahbicdee was puzzled.

"Baby, don't tell me you're getting cold feet on me?"

"Yeah baby, don't tell me you're getting cold feet," followed Coke.

"No, I'm not getting cold feet. It's just..."

"It's just what then?" she asked, uneasy.

"Yeah Dex, It's just what? C'mon and say it, break her heart," Coke instigated.

Dex closed his eyes, shaking his head.

"It's nothing. Listen Ahbicdee, go on in there to the party and meet your dad and his people. I'ma run along to one of these convenience stores and grab some drinks and gum. Don't want to go in there empty handed."

"Are your sure Dex?"

"Baby, I'm sure. I'll be back. Go ahead."

Ahbicdee exited the car. Dex waited until she entered the house and pulled off.

Coke in the passenger seat looked to Dex.

Dex

"Man, when are you gonna get some balls? You've waited for this moment almost your entire life and you're letting it go over a skirt? P' lease..."

"I love that woman Coke. You just don't understand. I've been waiting for her my whole life as well."

Coke pretended to yawn. "Save that shit for the choir, Dex. I know your black-ass. We're one, have you forgot? I'm you, and you're me. You just feel that way right now, but what about six months from now? Will you still feel the same way? Will you still tingle when she enters the room? Will her soft touch be enough to soothe that anger? Or, will her sex be the only sex you desire."

Dex appeared to be in thought about his answer.

"Hell naw!" Coke answered for him. "And you're a lie if you say it will. Be true to yourself Dex. Ahbicdee's like any other woman. Here today, gone tomorrow."

"It's not like that this time Coke. Ahbicdee's different."

"In the beginning, they're all different. After a while, they're something else. Be true to yourself Dex. Turn this car around and go back."

Dex hated how Coke was so persuasive. He hated how Coke was so involved in every equation of his life. But he knew Coke was right. Dex turned the car around and proceeded back to Naamens St.

When he arrived, he briefly sat thinking about what he was going to say, when he walked up to the door. He had no idea.

"Fuck it," hopping out of the car, walking onto the porch, ringing the doorbell.

An older gentle man answered the door. "What's going on fella? Can I help you?"

Nasty D!ck

Dex scanned over the man's perfectly trimmed, salt and pepper colored beard, his coffee stained teeth and his inward pointed eyebrows, making it appear he was upset. Dex handed him the crumbled letter from his pocket.

"Dex! I'm Claude," shaking his hand.

Dex stood hesistant.

"Well, don't just stand there. C'mon in. Let me introduce you to everybody."

Dex stepped inside the 4000 square foot home. It was nice with high ceilings, open rooms and large windows. Claude called everyone into the living room. As they entered, he began calling out their names.

"Here, you have Halice and Patrice, the twins," he introduced.

The twins waved.

"On the couch, that's Candace."

"Hi," Candace spoke.

"Over there," directing his finger across the room. "Is Marcus, Robert, Claude Jr. and his kids, Cameron, McGee, and Joshua, just Josh for short. And... Where is she?" looking around the room. "Where's Ahbi...? Oh, there she is."

Ahbicdee came walking from out the kitchen.

"And that's Ahbicdee," he lastly pointed out to Dex.

"Dex, that's everybody. Everybody, this is Dex, your brother from Detroit."

Dex began receiving handshakes, hugs and kisses from his never before seen siblings.

Brother! Ahbicdee's smile turned upside down. Black and white twilight swirls appeared in her eyes. She began to gasp as if she was having a heart attack, like an outer body experience.

"Ahbicdee's chokin'!"

Dex

Everyone rushed to her aid.

"Get her some water!"

"What's the matter with her?" voiced her brothers and sisters with concern.

Dex stood back. He knew there was nothing he could say to fix this with Ahbicdee. Not one thing.

Coke laughed himself silly. "Dex, did you see that look on Ahbicdee's face? Oh shit! That was Priceless."

Dex walked away, out the front door. He felt like shit.

Claude, his father, came running out behind him. "Dex!" he called. "Dex, wait!"

Dex turned around as Claude approached.

"Son, you just got here. Why are you leaving?" he asked short winded.

Dex had no answer that he wanted to explain. He hunched his shoulders. "I don't know why."

Claude placed his hand on his son's shoulder.

"Dex, I haven't been a father, parent or much of anything to you worth claiming. But I sent you and Ahbicdee a letter to be here to explain my actions, or I should I say my sickness? Son, let me ask you a question, and I want you to answer me honestly. Have you ever heard voices in your head, like a second person is talking to you or trying to control your actions, anything like that?"

"Don't you answer that damn question!" said Coke.

"Yes," Dex shook his head.

"And is that voice talking to you right now son?"

"Yes he is."

"What is he saying?"

"He's saying, 'Fuck you Claude, you sorry excuse of a man. Dex is with me now.'"

Nasty D!ck

Claude shook his head giving Dex a pill to take. He told Dex it would temporarily suppress his other personality while they talked. Dex took the pill and immediately felt his cloudy thoughts clearing up. He hadn't felt this mind free in thirty years.

Claude began explaining to Dex how he as a young man, noticed signs of his split personality; ending up in places having no idea of how he'd gotten there; waking up laying next to women he didn't remember meeting; and the worst, fathering children unable to remember when he conceived them. "Shit, for all I know, these women could've been lying on me."

"Well, were they?"

"Nah, what woman in her right mind would claim a dead beat dad to be her child's father if he wasn't. I got eleven children by ten different women. That other side of me had some whorish ways."

"It sure did." cosigned Dex. *And I thought I was bad with my seven children and six different mothers. I guess the apple don't fall too far from the tree.* "But why did you leave me behind?" Dex wanted to know. "I was just a little boy. I waited for you."

"I'm sorry Dex. I had no control over my behavior. One minute I was sanely there, and the next I was mentally gone. Barbara knew I wasn't right. She asked me not to come back until I received help. And the same thing happen with Cynthia, Ahbicdee's mother. She too didn't want our daughter witnessing me change into these different personalities. Besides, juggling two families was rough. I was spending time over here, spending time over there. Everyday, I'd lie to keep the lie straight. On top of being the caring family man that I was, that vicious, I don't give a fuck

Dex

side of me kept coming out. I had no choice but to leave you behind son. I needed help."

Dex looked up the street, feeling that was no excuse for his father's thirty-year absents. He then looked back to his father asking, "What about your other kids in there referring to his brother and sisters. "Were you in their lives?'

"Same story, Dex. They were brought up no different by me than you were, except they were born and raised here in Chicago."

"But you just finished saying you left Detroit because you needed some help."

"I said I needed help. I didn't say I received any."

Dex lip hung with dismay. "So why are you standing here feeding me all this bullshit, Claude? I'd respect it more if you'd just admit that you were a deadbeat dad to me and we move on. No matter what you say, we can't get those thirty years back, so keep it real."

Claude stood offended from Dex's choice of words. But he realized his son was right. No matter the excuse, they could never recapture the past thirty years. Claude apologized to Dex for not being there as a father.

After clearing the air, he spoke to his son about the suppressant he had given to him earlier. He explained the pill was experimental, effective, but not yet approved by the F.D.A. (Food and Drug Administration). He claimed years of testing and billions of dollars had been put towards this cure, further stating additional subjects with the mental disorder, schizophrenia were needed.

"They need people like you," Claude pointed to Dex.

Dex's forehead wrinkled. "Why me? Why don't you be a test dummy?"

"I already am. That's how I know the pills works." Claude grabbed Dex by the shoulders. "Son, you're young, strong, and you have all the behavioral symptoms. You're perfect for this program. Not to mention, they pay well too. How do you think I got this big house?"

Dex was in thought. *This muthafucka' Claude ain't nothin' but a hustler. I can hear it all up in his voice. I waited thirty long years for this? This man doesn't love me. He don't give a fuck about me. This here invite is about money to line his pockets up. He wants to use my illness for his own financial gain. Dex smirked looking towards the ground. Claude hasn't earned the right to call me his son. He just doesn't know. Game recognizes game.*

Claude continued. "So, are you in son?" extending his hand. Dex looked at his father's hand wanting to spit in it, but embraced it for a shake.

"Yeah, I'm in. But you gotta be honest with me about the health risks and the side effects."

"Not to worry Dex, you'll be well informed."

Just as the two released from their handshake, Ahbicdee came walking out of the house, appearing to have made a full recovery. As she approached, Dex sighed knowing he was about to be fronted off.

"Daddy," she called sweetly kissing her father on the cheek. "Are you and Dex going to stand here talking all day, or are you going to come back inside and join the reunion?" To Dex surprise, she gave him no fuss or fight. *Ahbicdee might be cool with this thing,* he thought.

"We were just finishing up darling. May I escort you back inside?" Claude asked bending his arm.

Ahbicdee folded her arm around his.

"Yes you may."

Dex, standing on the other side of her bent his arm as well.

Ahbicdee rolled her eyes ignoring him.

Dex

"C'mon daddy." She and Claude then headed back inside the house.

Dex remained standing on the sidewalk. *I'm sorry baby,* hanging his head.

Inside the house, everyone was dancing, laughing, eating, drinking, and just having a good time. Dex tried to get into the groove, but his mind was heavy on Ahbicdee, who hadn't made any eye contact with him one time tonight.

Finally, Dex managed to get close enough to her to whisper in her ear. "Let me talk to you for a minute," several times he asked, only to be ignored. He then suddenly pretended to be drunk, snatching Ahbicdee by the arm, steering her into the backyard. Now face-to-face, "What the hell is the problem? You've been ignoring me all night!"

Ahbicdee looked side to side as if to say, *Are you serious?* She started off aggressively sticking her finger in Dex face. "Ignoring you? Muthafucka'! I should be trying to kill you. Just yesterday, you were my lover, now today I find out you're my brother? How sick is that Dex? This is the twenty-first century. Shit like this doesn't happen anymore. You knew you nasty dick bastard. You knew we were related."

Dex was shaking his head, *No.*

"Don't lie. Yes you did. I showed you the letter daddy sent to me after the first time we had sex. You're eyes widened when you read his name. I didn't think anything of it then, but now I know. You were sent the same letter from Claude. The sick thing about it is; you fucked me this morning knowing I was your sister. You're just a nasty dick bastard Dex. It's the only way to describe you. Then in the car, you talking about how you don't want to enter the party empty handed, and you were going to the store. My question to you Dex, is why didn't you just keep on going? Why didn't you just hop back on a flight to Detroit? Why didn't you try to protect my feelings," with tears rolling down her face. "You know about almost everything I've been through. You even know my current situation with my husband. Are you trying to destroy me, Dex? Is that what you want, to tear me down? This was supposed to be one of the happiest days of my life; being reunited with my father, my brothers and sisters, and my nieces and nephews, who I've never met. But instead, I'm hurting. My heart aches. I just can't figure out what I've done in this life to deserve such a raw deal," crying.

Dex tried to console Ahbicdee caressing her back. She cringed from his touch.

"Get your disgusting, wretched hands off of me!" snatching away, wiping her tears. "I'm done with letting filth like you run my life. I've been through so much bullshit, I can't help but to stand strong now. I've seen... You know what Dex, it doesn't even matter anymore. You're not worth the breath. I'm going back inside to enjoy my father and get acquainted with the rest of my family. Why don't you go lay in some gutter with the rest of the trash," walking away.

Dex grabbed her arm. "Baby, I still love you! We can make this work!"

"You should've thought about that before you came back here, Mr. Nasty Dick," again snatching away.

"Mmph, mmph, mmph. Ahbicdee dogged your ass out. And what she call you? Mr. Nasty Dick?" Coke laughed. "That's some funny shit. I told you Dex, they're here today, and gone tomorrow."

Dex said nothing, surprised Coke was even there. "Oh, and Dex. I'll let you in on a little secret. That pill you digested, it doesn't work. But you were right in your

Dex

thoughts. Ol' Claude just wants cash in on you're dysfunctional brain. He doesn't love you, never has. And your new lost love, siblings, they're in on it too. Ahbicdee, I think she genuinely had feelings for you, but that's now dead. Sorry to be the one who breaks it to you kid, but it's just you and me again, for life."

With that said, Dex felt alone. He felt betrayed and angered. Any love he had in his heart was turning into hate. That hate was fueling Coke further into existence, until Dex was no more.

"Ahh... Finally," cracking his neck side to side. "Now, time to get rid of some unwanted family members." Coke went from the backyard back inside to the reunion. He mingled, danced and toasted a drink to Claude. He then quietly slipped himself out the front door.

Coke rushed back to the hotel room, unzipping a hidden compartment in Dex suitcase, pulling out a small, plastic, green bottle with skull and crossbones on the label. He twisted the cap off the bottle catching the faint almond odor, Potassium Cyanide gave off.

"If nothing else, this will do it," slipping the bottle of poison into his pocket. He afterwards hurried back to the party. When Coke entered the house, Claude was on one knee in front of everyone apologizing to Ahbicdee, asking for her forgiveness for his absence in her life.

Perfect, thought Coke, seeing everyone was preoccupied. He slowly eased his way over to the punch bowl. "This is for the kids," pouring in half the bottle of poison, stirring it around. "And now, for the grown folks," pre-making alcoholic drinks.

As Ahbicdee gave her sentimental speech about what this reunion meant to her, Coke was passing out the drinks for a toast. Some took sips of their drink before the speech was over. Others downed their drink going back for seconds. When the speech ended, Coke was the first to put up his cup.

"To Ahbicdee!"

"To Ahbicdee!" Everyone else followed in unison. Coke watched with no heart or emotion as the tainted drinks quenched everyone's thirsts. Some smelled the insides of their cup catching the almond scent, but thought nothing of it.

Claude pointed to Coke. "Dex, is there anything you want to say to me or any of your brothers and sisters here today."

Coke at first was hesitant not realizing Claude was speaking to him, until the house focused their attention in his direction.

"Oh, yeah... Yeah, I got something I want to say," stepping to the center of the room.

"Claude, you've lived a long life, a long healthy life. You've been blessed as well. You have a nice home; you have all eleven of your children here, grandchildren. What more can a man ask for?"

Claude feeling glorification shook his head in response, *Nothing.*

Coke continued. "But there got to be something you want Claude. I mean, after thirty years, you're now just deciding to bring Ahbicdee and myself here for a visit? After thirty long years? That's bullshit Claude. Be honest, you want something."

"You don't talk to my daddy that way!" spoke one of the twins.

"Fuck you!" responded Coke. "This sack of shit standing here ain't yo' daddy, he just bust a nut to get you here, just as he did for the rest of y'all," pointing to the other brothers and sisters.

Dex

Right then Claude realized the man standing before him wasn't Dex, it was Coke. Claude grabbed him around the neck, but Coke slipped from his hold, giving Claude a two-punch combination to the chin. Claude fell hard to the floor.

"That muthafucka' done hit daddy!"

A swarm of fists caved in on Coke's world. He fought back, but soon found himself curled into a ball on the floor being kicked and stomped.

Ahbicdee covered her mouth, dropping her drink never taking a sip. She couldn't believe what was going on. *Oh my God! Dex is ruining the reunion,* now looking to her father who was convulsing, seeming to be having a heart attack. She along with her sisters rushed to his side.

Coke on the floor felt the kicks and blows lessoning. When he looked up, a few of his attackers were laying on the floor shaking and foaming at their mouths. Another brother claimed of dizziness trying to make it out of the front door for help. Coke jumped off the floor. He ran over, tackling him by the waist.

The whole house seemed to be getting sick before Ahbicdee's eyes. She screamed in a panic.

"Oh my God! They're throwing up! Dex, what did you do to them? What was in those drinks?" knowing he somehow was responsible. She pulled out her cell phone to call 911. Coke slapped it from her hand.

"Get the fuck off the phone!"

"What are you doing Dex? Our father's dying!"

"Dying? Dying? Shit, ol' Claude's dead," kicking him. "He's already done been through the motions; foaming of the mouth, increased heart rate, respiratory failure and a lack of oxygen to his heart and brain, which ultimately lead to his death. Don't you just love a well thought out murder plan?" pulling a plastic baggie from his back pocket.

Ahbicdee began to back away.

"You crazy bastard, Dex! What's the matter with you?"

"The name's Coke, Ahbicdee, Coke. Remember that, so after I kill your ass, you can tell them who sent you."

No more needed to be said, Ahbicdee tried to run towards the front door. Coke blocked her path. She then redirected her way into the kitchen grabbing the biggest knife she could find. Coke was coming up behind her as she swung the knife with all of her might. He jumped back, missing him only by inches. She clenched her teeth.

"C'mon you muthafucka' who ever you are! This gon' be the hardest kill you ever make."

"Well, I'm up for the challenge," said Coke, with the plastic bag open in his hand. "Are you?"

"Step a little closer and find out."

There was a long two minute eye-to-eye standoff between the two. Ahbicdee with the knife tight in her hand knew something had to give. She tried to compromise the situation.

"Listen Dex, Coke, or whoever you are. Just let me walk out of this house, and I promise you, I won't say a thing."

Coke acted as if he was considering the thought. "Nah, I don't think so. I want to see that look of shock in your eyes when I wrap this bag around your face. I want to hear you moan, kick, fight and scratch for your precious life. I want to see the condensation from your hot breath inside the bag, as you struggle to breathe. Finally, I want my face to be the last image trapped in your cold dead eyes, just like Ché's."

Dex

"Ché! What about her?"

Coke hunched. "I bagged her ass, and that unfaithful husband of yours too; couldn't keep his dick at home to save his life. The way I see it Ahbicdee, you should be thanking me."

Ahbicdee stomped in a desperate rage.

"No! No! No! Please...! Just let me go!"

Coke had enough. He was now jumping at Ahbicdee, threatening to attack. Ahbicdee defensively kept swinging the knife knowing she was running out of time. She quickly scanned every part of the kitchen, making her way over to the stove. There, she grabbed a pot of cooking grease and doused it across the floor. Coke stepped backwards avoiding the grease. Ahbicdee found more cooking oil in another cabinet. She opened it and poured it onto the floor, creating even more space between them.

Coke was in thought. *This bitch has a brain in her head.* He pointed in frustrated. "I hope you don't think this little plan of yours is gon' stop me!"

"Obviously, it's doing something. I'm over here, and you're over there," smearing the grease along the floor with a broom. She soon painted herself into a corner in the kitchen.

"What are you gon' do now, Ms. Smart Bitch? You done trapped yourself."

Ahbicdee agreed, again looking around the kitchen, noticing she was standing next to a box of can goods. She opened the box and began hurling the cans at the kitchen window. Suddenly, Crash! A can went through the window.

"Help! Please! Somebody, help!" she screamed.

"Hey! Cut it out! Stop that screaming! I'ma kill you!"

Nasty D!ck

Just then, Ahbicdee threw a can striking Coke on the bridge of his nose. He grabbed his face, tears streamed from his eyes.

"Oh you bitch!" he squealed in pain, wiping the blood streaming on both sides of his nose.

She continued hollering. "Help...! Help...! Please...! Somebody!"

But before Ahbicdee knew it, Coke was hauling ass towards her like he was on dry a surface. He screamed in rage as he approached. Ahbicdee timed him. Only inches from his reach, she suddenly used the dry floor to propel herself out of his way. Coke crashed into the wall, falling to the floor.

Ahbicdee's feet were in fast motion, but going nowhere quick, slipping and sliding on the oily surface. She was so scared her legs were like rubber, not looking back one time. Her eyes were focused on getting to that dry carpet.

As she neared the carpet, the excitement of escape overtook her, suddenly finding both of her feet in the air, landing onto her back. Blam!

A second later, Coke pounced on top of Ahbicdee wrapping the plastic bag around her face. The bag around her neck was so tight, she could feel her eyes filling with blood. The pressure made her head feel as if it were going to explode. Her life was slipping away. She felt herself dying, but Ahbicdee wasn't going out without a fight. She moaned, kicked, fought and scratched for her precious life, just as Coke said she would, until surprisingly, the bag loosened up.

Ahbicdee gasped for air, tearing the plastic from around her face. She was so grateful to be alive, appreciative for air. She then looked to her attacker who was lying stiff, with the handle of the knife lodged into his chest. It appeared

Dex

Coke had been stabbed through the heart. His eyes were open, but his heart beat was slow. The nerves in his fingers twitched. Death took its time, but eventually moved in. Ahbicdee carefully took a closer look into his face, watching, as his pupils went dark. She was the last image in his cold dead eyes.

"One, two, three," snap! "One, two, three," snap! Patient's not responding to my awakening signal. He's still in the hypnosis state," said Dr. Barton. "Call in the nurse."

Just then, Dex lying on the patients couch opened his eyes. He frantically jumped up. "Where's Ahbicdee?"

"Who?" asked Dr. Barton.

"Ahbicdee! My girlfriend! I have to save her from Coke!" standing to his feet.

Dr. Barton nodded. The orderlies restrained Dex back into the chair.

"Let me go! Ahbicdee's in danger!"

Dr. Barton closed his eyes and shook his head.

"Dex, I really hoped that you were getting better. I told you before. There is no Ahbicdee, no Ché, Flower, Ocknock, Coke, or the others. None of these people exist, only in your head."

"They do exist dammit! They're all real! Get the fuck off of me!" struggling with the orderlies.

Dr. Barton pointed to the nurse. "Beverly here will give you something to calm your nerves."

Dex was injected with a shot. He slowly began to nod. When he finally went to sleep, he was hauled off back to his room.

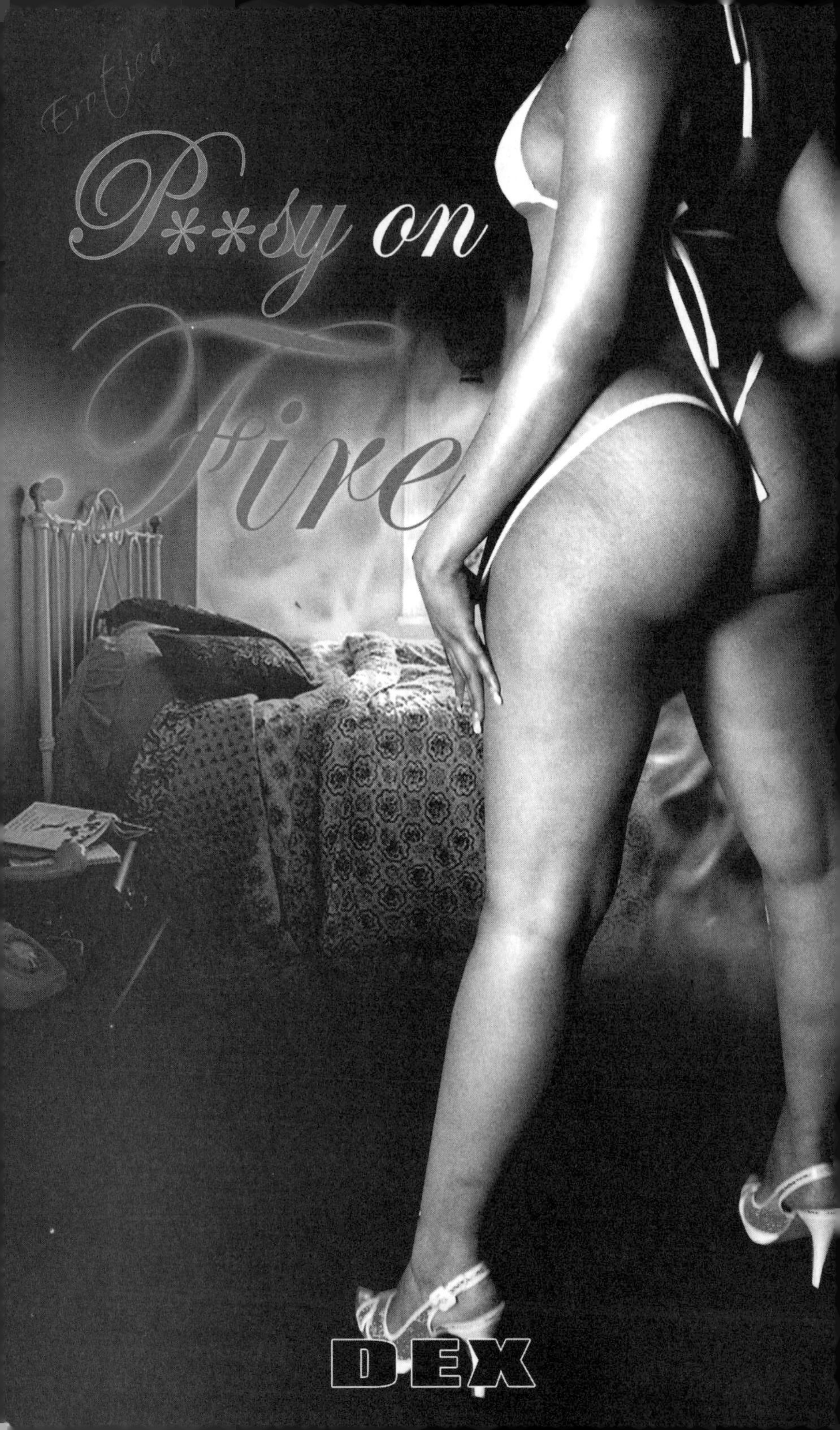
Erotica
P**sy on
Fire
DEX

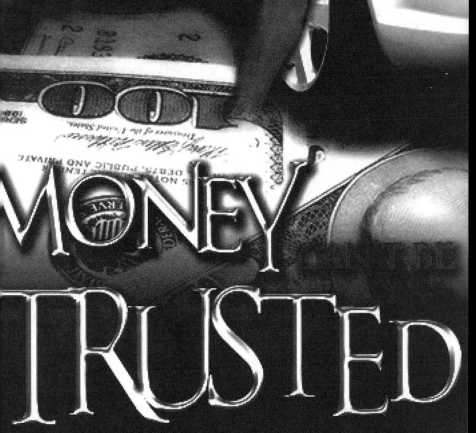

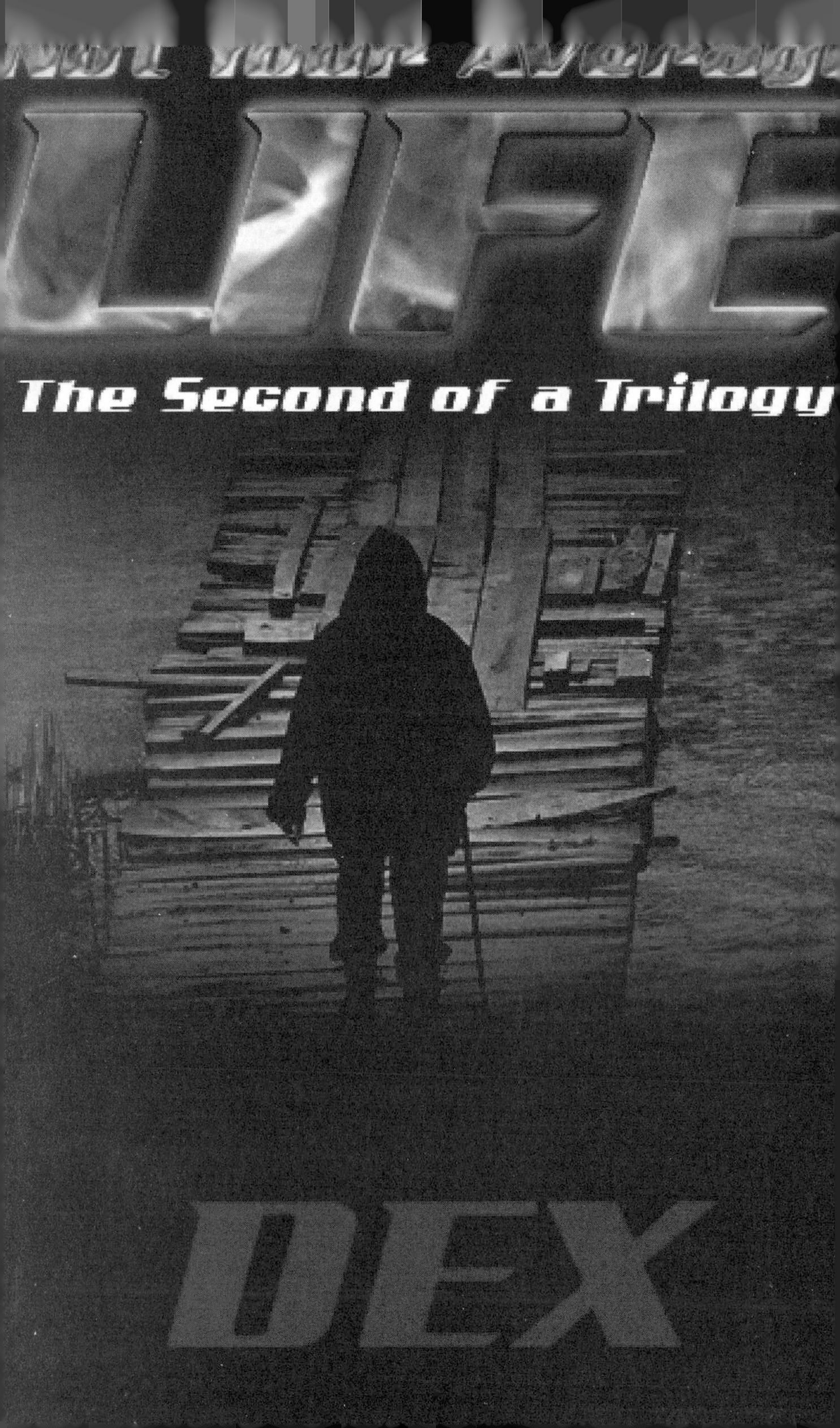
LIFE
The Second of a Trilogy
DEX